A Reason for Living

BY LYNN STANLEY

NAVPRESS ●®
A MINISTRY OF THE NAVIGATORS
P.O. BOX 6000, COLORADO SPRINGS, COLORADO 80934

The Navigators is an international Christian organization. Jesus Christ gave His followers the Great Commission to go and make disciples (Matthew 28:19). The aim of The Navigators is to help fulfill that commission by multiplying laborers for Christ in every nation.

NavPress is the publishing ministry of The Navigators. NavPress publications are tools to help Christians grow. Although publications alone cannot make disciples or change lives, they can help believers learn biblical discipleship, and apply what they learn to their lives and ministries.

Cover art: Michael Garland

All Scripture quotations in this publication are from the *Holy Bible: New International Version* (NIV). Copyright © 1973, 1978, 1984, International Bible Society. Used by permission of Zondervan Bible Publishers.

Printed in the United States of America

For Fred, Tracie, and B. J.

"A happy family is but an earlier heaven."
—Sir John Bowring

[God] will wipe every tear from their eyes. There will be no more death or mourning or crying or pain, for the old order of things has passed away.

REVELATION 21:4

CHAPTER ONE

Beau Collins burst through the front door of the huge Santa-Barbara-style mansion. "Trish?" he called frantically. "Trish, are you here? Answer me!" When she didn't answer, a feeling of panic grabbed him, choking him like hands around his throat.

He charged up the enormous staircase, taking the steps two and three at a time, until breathlessly, he reached the landing at the top. He paused, caught his breath, and called again: "Trish, are you up here?" No answer.

Running to the end of the long hallway, he found the doors to the master suite ajar. Hopeful, he looked inside, but he saw no one. He checked the master bath, the dressing room, and finally, the enormous wardrobe closet. Trish was nowhere in sight.

Beau turned on his heel and hurried back down the hallway, thrusting doors open as he went and calling into each room: "Trish? Trish, answer me!" He stood still, straining to hear even the faintest sound from some distant room. There was only silence. Suddenly, fear shone like a devil's mask on his face. He turned abruptly and charged down the staircase. He ran through the huge drawing room into the dining room through the kitchen and out the door into the back yard. Then, Beau Collins gasped in horror as he saw Trish's dead body, floating face down in the swimming pool.

Her lifeless arms were outstretched, while the exquisite evening gown formed bugle-beaded billows around her body. Her thick auburn hair—always perfectly done—floated like spider's legs around her head.

There was not a sound as a wispy breeze sent palm fronds dancing gracefully against the starlit sky. The moonlight cast shadows on his handsome face as Beau Collins stood—perfectly attired in white dinner jacket and black-silk bow tie—and stared at the body of his dead lover.

His strong jaw never quivered. His crystal-blue eyes never teared. Not one curly black hair on his gorgeous head even moved as Beau turned dramatically and looked up at the broken balcony. . . . *Trish Tyler had been pushed!* A haunting musical theme began to swell, signaling the end of the program.

Holly Henderson jumped up, aimed the remote control directly at the television, then pushed the "off" button violently. "It serves her right!" she said out loud to no one in particular. "That witch was bound to get it sooner or later!"

She reset the timer on the VCR so that it would be ready to tape the next day's show. Since her dad first took the part of Beau Collins almost six years ago, Holly hadn't missed a single episode.

It was dinner time. Holly felt hungry, but she didn't

8

feel like cooking. More than that, she didn't feel like sitting at the dinner table alone again. She had eaten dinner by herself every night since her mother took the job at the radio station.

Holly went to the kitchen and searched the refrigerator, finally settling for a lonesome carrot and a bottle of beer. She plopped down by the phone and, between chomps, dialed Lindsey's number.

"Hello?"

"Hey, Lins, what's up?" She chuckled, glancing at the large orange vegetable in her hand. "I'm sitting here eating a carrot, and all of a sudden, I'm starting to sound like Bugs Bunny!"

"Hi, Holly! I'm trying to figure out this stupid algebra. I swear, this is the most useless junk I'll never learn! When am I ever going to use this stuff?"

"Beats me. Wanna go out?"

"Out where?"

"I don't care. The Fantastic, maybe."

"The Fantastic? Are you crazy? You know I can't go dancing on a school night. As a matter of fact, you can't either!"

"No one's going to know, dummy. We're gonna sneak out."

"Sneak out? Are you crazy?"

"No, I'm not crazy! Just climb out the window and meet me at The Fantastic. We'll be home by 10:30 or 11:00. No one will know. . . ."

"You're nuts! My mom will kill me if she finds out!"

"She won't find out! My mom never finds out."

"Well, your mom's been working every night. *My* mom'll find out. My mother *always* finds out!"

9

"Oh, come on, Lins, you're such a *stiff*!"

"Look, Holly, after that last stunt you talked me into, I'm lucky I still have a room to call my own!"

Holly pretended shock. "Why, Lindsey Anna Marshall, I can't believe you'd say a thing like that! After all, you have a free will—no one *made* you set that bag of dog droppings on fire and put it on Heidi Wagner's doorstep."

"Well, it was *your* idea!"

"Yeah, but *you* did it." Visualizing the prank, both girls laughed. "You gotta admit, Lins, it was great! I'll never forget the look on Heidi's face when she stomped on the bag to put out the flames and the dog-do splattered all over her shoes!"

Lindsey's voice was edged with sarcasm: "Yeah, it was a riot, all right—until her father pulled in the driveway and caught us laughing hysterically behind the bushes! And it was a scream and a half when Mrs. Wagner called our parents, and you and I had to sit on the front porch and clean the dog-do off Heidi's shoes while her mother delivered a lecture on kindness to others. I thought my mom would kill me when I got home!"

"She might as well have. She grounded you for two weeks. You gotta admit it was worth it, though."

"Yeah, I admit that, all right. It stopped Heidi from snitching on us for passing notes in science."

"Well, are you gonna sneak out with me tonight, or are you going to stay home and vegetate with your algebra?"

Lindsey hesitated. "I don't know. . . . My folks are right downstairs. What if they check my room?"

"Go tell them you're tired, you're just going to finish

your homework and go to bed early. Then go back upstairs, turn out your light and put pillows under your blanket—they'll think you're asleep under the covers."

"Well . . . okay, I'll meet you at The Fantastic at eight!"

"Atta girl!"

Holly hung up and checked her watch. She hurried to her room and turned on the radio, changing the dial from the rock station to WTLK. She turned the volume way up so she wouldn't miss anything and hopped into the shower as the "For Parents Only" program began. She listened intently as Dr. Carol announced the topic for the evening's program: "Building Your Child's Self-Esteem." After a short discussion on the topic, Dr. Carol cautioned callers to be patient—the phone lines were already jammed with concerned parents in need of advice. She broke for a commercial just as Holly jumped out of the shower.

Quickly, Holly wrapped herself in a towel and dialed the radio station. She received a cold, impersonal greeting. "WTLK Talk Radio," the voice said.

"Frank, this is Holly. I need to talk to my mom."

He tapped on the window of the sound booth and motioned for Dr. Carol Henderson to pick up the phone.

Her face brightened when she heard Holly's voice. "Hi, pumpkin!"

"Hi, Mom. I just called to say good night."

Holly's mom glanced at the large clock on the wall. "At 7:15?" she said skeptically.

"I'm really tired. I'm just going to finish my homework and go to bed early." She felt guilty about lying, but not too guilty.

11

"Good girl! Well, I'm glad you called—I was going to check with you later. Did Pops call?"

"No, I guess he forgot."

"Did you watch the show?"

"Yeah. It was starting to drag again but they juiced it up: Trish finally got hers. Someone knocked her fancy little carcass off the balcony into the pool!"

"It's about time!" she laughed. "How was Dad?"

"He was great! He looked really handsome. He had on a white dinner jacket with a pink carnation for the last scene. I'm gonna miss Trish, though. She was such a great character, so *mean!*"

"Well, don't worry about it. She'll be back. Remember two years ago? They killed her off in the car crash, and she came back as her twin sister."

"Yeah."

"Holly, I've got the most exciting news! They're thinking of giving me my own show—*permanently!*"

If Holly's mom had been in the same room with her daughter, she would have seen the look of horror on Holly's face. "I thought this was only temporary?" Holly said.

"Well, it was, but the ratings are so good they're thinking of continuing my show even after Dr. Highland comes back from vacation! Isn't that great?"

"No, it's not great! You're never home! I never see you any more. It's bad enough with Dad home only on weekends. I can't take it in this big house all alone every night!"

Holly's mom was aghast. This was hardly the response she expected. "Holly, I can't believe you feel this way. Surely you must understand what this means to my career! And the money is nothing to shake a stick at, either."

"We don't need more money, Mom," Holly said flatly. "I miss you! I never see you."

Her voice softened. "Oh, honey, of course you do. I'm sorry. It's just that this is such a great opportunity for me. . . . I never thought you'd react this way. You're sixteen years old. Most kids your age would *love* the opportunity for a little freedom."

Holly had to admit that if her mom were home, she wouldn't have enjoyed a carrot and a bottle of beer for dinner. And it would be a lot harder to sneak out at night. It could be done, but it would be much more difficult! "Well," she reasoned thoughtfully, "maybe we shouldn't worry about it until it happens."

"That's a good idea. It's only a possibility, anyway."

The producer gave Dr. Carol a signal indicating that there were less than thirty seconds left before air time. She acknowledged him with a wave of her hand. "Listen, honey, I gotta run. I've got six phone lines backed up here. . . ."

Holly hung up the phone and rehashed the conversation with her mother. She'd just die if her mother got her own show! Things had been awful lately, with both of her parents gone most of the time. She missed her after-dinner talks with her mother, and she never had anyone to help her with homework. When something exciting happened at school, there was no one to share it with. But worst of all, there was just no one to *be* with.

She stomped down the stairs to the kitchen and jerked open the refrigerator door. She took another bottle of beer, opened it, and threw the bottle opener against the wall. She emptied the bottle in two long swallows.

The more time her mother spent at the radio station, the further they drifted apart. It was as if Holly were all alone in her world and her parents were someplace else, altogether. Now, if her mother got her own radio show in addition to her private practice. . . .

Holly snapped the idea from her head. She couldn't worry about that now. She had dancing to do.

CHAPTER TWO

Loud rock music pulsed through the outside speakers and into the parking lot at The Fantastic, calling every kid in the neighborhood to come over and dance. The girls greeted each other with a hug. "You look great!" Holly said.

Lindsey posed with one hand on the back of her head and the other on her hip, and then she turned full circle. "Yes, I do, don't I?"

Holly slugged her playfully. "What about me? How do I look?"

Lindsey surveyed her best friend's clothes carefully. Holly's skirt was two inches longer than those in fashion. "I suppose that was your mother's skirt when she was in high school?" She knew her friend's fondness for things of the past.

"Yeah, isn't it great? Don't you love the colors? I love the combination—red, blue, purple—and isn't this print *wild*?" She lifted the hem of the skirt, fan-style, so Lindsey could get a better look.

"It's different," Lindsey said, not sure if she liked it

or not. Next, she examined Holly's shoes. They were the same red as in the skirt, open-toed, with ankle straps and low heels. They were very different from anything any of the other girls wore, but Lindsey wasn't sure if they were out of style, or just not *in* yet. Holly wore a bright-purple oversized sweater belted at the hips, and a brightly colored wooden necklace with every kind of fruit imaginable hanging loosely around her neck. She had dangling earrings to match (bananas and grapes, apples and oranges). Her long ash-blonde hair was pulled up into a ponytail and tied with a purple nylon scarf. Long bangs hung over her eyebrows, and loose, wispy strands of hair framed her almost perfect face. Her smile was radiant as she waited for her friend's approval.

"You're strange. . . . But you look *fabulous*!"

"I'll take that as a compliment. I think."

The Fantastic was packed every Wednesday night because girls got in free. Colored lights flashed wildly, as loud rock music vibrated through speakers placed strategically around the dance floor. Holly took Lindsey by the hand and pulled her through the crowd.

They heard a voice shouting over the noise: "Holly! Hey, Holly! Over here!"

She turned to see Kevin waving his arms over his head. They walked to the table where he sat with several other kids. "Hey, Kevin, what's happening?" She looked the group over. "Hi, Sandy, you look great! Hi, Dave! Where's Billy?"

"Aw, he's in the john," Kevin said. "He drank a six-pack and a half bottle of cheap wine before we came. Now he's talkin' to Ralph."

"Ralph? Ralph who?"

"You know . . . Ral-l-l-p-h-h-h!" He doubled over, grabbed his stomach, and pretended to throw up. "Hey, ya wanna little swallow?" He reached inside his jacket, pulled out a small bottle of bourbon, and offered it to the girls in secret.

Lindsey waved him off, but Holly took a long sip and then grabbed Kevin by the hand. "Let's dance!"

As they moved erratically to the music, Kevin shouted over the noise: "You snuck out again, didn't you?"

"Yeah."

"How do you keep doing it and never get caught?"

"My mom's been working nights the last few weeks."

"Oh yeah! My dad heard the show."

When Lindsey jerked Holly's arm and pulled her off the dance floor, Kevin went right on dancing. "Jeff's here!" she said, pointing to a group of boys in the corner.

"Oh my gosh. Do you think he might ask one of us to dance? Preferably *me*."

The two girls looked hopeful. But the hope faded when Jeff moved, and they saw Cindy Aldrich standing directly behind him. Lindsey's smile disappeared. "Forget it. Cindy's here."

"We should have known better than to think she'd let him come to a place like this without her! Oh," she whined, stomping her foot, "I just want to *dance* with him!"

Cindy noticed them looking over and smiled sweetly as she put her arms around Jeff's waist and snuggled

17

close to him, resting her head on his chest.

"Doesn't that just about make you wanna puke?" Lindsey said.

"Yeah. She might as well have a flashing neon sign on her forehead: 'He's mine—He's mine—He's mine'!"

"What does he see in her, anyway? She's such a *snot!*"

"Now, be nice!" Holly cautioned. "You don't know she's a snot. . . ."

"Mary Elizabeth O'Donnell told me she was. And if Mary Elizabeth says so, it's true. She *never* lies!"

"Oh, Cindy's probably all right once you get to know her."

"That's what they said about Jack the Ripper! Besides, she wouldn't give the time of day to a lowly, slimy little sophomore!"

Holly studied her friend carefully. Lindsey was an exceptionally good judge of character, but in this case, Holly thought she was wrong. No one as nice as Jeff Reynolds would go with a girl as mean as Lindsey described.

"Everyone hates her," Lindsey continued. "She's so stuck up it's pathetic! Look at her, she hangs on him like a cheap suit! She won't even let him *dance* with anyone!" She stared for a moment, and then added, "You have to admit, she's pretty. There's not one single thing wrong with her face. It's not fair that someone can be so mean and look so good!"

"I can't believe she's as bad as everyone says, or she wouldn't be going with someone as sweet as Jeff."

"That's because he doesn't know her like we do! She's the most two-faced person I've ever known!"

18

The truth was, Lindsey didn't know Cindy at all. She had never even *talked* to her. Very few people actually *knew* Cindy Aldrich, but everyone thought they did because she was head cheerleader and had her picture on nearly every page of the yearbook.

"Why do you say she's two-faced?"

"Well, for one thing, Brenda Melroy's supposed to be her best friend, right?"

"Yeah."

"Well, Cindy has math in 203 right before I do. I sit at her desk. One day, she left a note on the desk that she'd written to Susan. Cindy told Susan that Brenda would never win homecoming queen because her thighs are too fat!"

Holly considered this disloyalty carefully. She and Lindsey would never do anything like that to each other. In fact, in all the time they'd known each other, they had never had a hateful word between them.

". . . And what about what she did to Mary Elizabeth? Mary had that job at Confetti's sewn up!"

Confetti's was a clothing store in the mall that carried all the latest fashions and accessories. They paid well, had great sales, and gave a generous discount to their employees. They always had a waiting list for jobs, so it was nearly impossible to get one.

"Cindy stole that job right from under Mary's nose!"

"You don't know that for sure."

"Oh, don't I? Well, it just so happens that Mary told me, and she *never* lies!"

"I know. You just told me that," Holly reminded her. "What happened?"

19

"When Gwen quit, she told Mary so she could get first crack at the job. She even told the manager she was sending a friend in—meaning Mary, of course. Mary was talking to Cindy and mentioned all this to her, telling her how nice Gwen had been and all. When Mary was at pep club after school, Cindy rushed to Confetti's first! She told the manager that she was a friend of Gwen's, and he just assumed Cindy was the one Gwen sent in, so he hired her instead!"

"That's *awful!*" Holly said.

"You better believe it's awful. Mary needed that job! Cindy didn't even want it. She quit three weeks later, but by then, Mary had a job at Food City.

"Cindy does all that rotten stuff, and then she gets a terrific boyfriend like Jeff Reynolds, and no one else can even dance with him! It's just not fair!" Lindsey protested.

"She's voted class princess *and* cheerleader every single year," Holly said. "If she's so mean, why does she win everything?"

"We *both* know why she always wins everything!"

"We do?"

"Well, of course, silly!" Lindsey grew serious, as if she were about to explain Einstein's Theory of Relativity. "Over half the students at Kennedy are boys, right?"

"Right."

Lindsey threw her hands up—a visual proclamation that she had solved the puzzle. "Look at her! Look at that hair! Look at that face and that body! Men vote with their *eyes*, not their *brains!*"

Holly guessed she'd known that all along, but just

hadn't thought about it. "I still can't believe she's that bad. . . . If she were *that* bad, Jeff wouldn't like her."

"While I was in the bathroom between classes yesterday, Brenda and Susan were talking about Jeff and Cindy," Lindsey offered excitedly. "They didn't know I was in there. Anyway, Brenda told Susan that Jeff broke up with Cindy, and Cindy was making a total fool of herself because she can't accept the fact that he doesn't like her anymore. Brenda said that Cindy calls him about a hundred times a day and follows him like a shadow!"

"Well, if he *did* break up with her, he must have changed his mind, because they look pretty much like a couple to me."

"That's just because he's so nice he probably doesn't want to hurt her feelings in public."

Holly smiled at her friend. "You've got all the answers, don't you? Oh, well," she said matter-of-factly, "we'll find someone else to dance with. There are other fish."

"Yeah, but all these other guys are catfish compared to Jeff." Her eyes grew dreamy. "He's a . . . blue marlin!"

Holly wrinkled her nose. "That's the smelliest metaphor I've ever heard!"

They watched as Jeff took Cindy's hand and led her onto the dance floor. A ballad was playing, and the disc jockey dimmed the lights. A large ball covered with tiny mirrored squares dropped down from the ceiling and began turning slowly. Its motion sent romantic sparkles of light dancing playfully on the walls and floor. Lindsey tried to imagine herself in Cindy's place as Jeff held her close, smiling and talking sweetly into her ear.

"Aren't they the most perfect-looking couple you could imagine?" she asked.

"No. The most perfect couple I could imagine is Jeff and *me*," Holly said truthfully.

"Fat chance!"

"Stranger things have happened."

"I know. I heard about a baby who was born with a beard!" Lindsey offered.

Holly was genuinely surprised. "No kidding? That *is* strange! Well, before the night's over, you'll see Jeff and me dancing—together."

There was a tap on Holly's arm. It was Billy. He slurred words at her, "Wanna dansh?"

She laughed out loud, teasing him. "I don't know how to 'dansh,' Billy. But if you'd like to *dance*, I'd love to—if you promise not to step on my new shoes."

"It'sh a deal," he said weakly.

Another slow song was playing, and Billy attempted to push Holly around the floor. "You're fun," he said.

"You're a real barrel of monkeys yourself."

"No, Holly, I mean it! You're one of the funnest . . . no, *the funnest* girl in our whole school. Everyone says so. You're the prettiest, too." He stepped back and examined her, scratching his head thoughtfully. "No, that's not true. *Cindy's* the prettiest, but she's a snot. I asked her to dansh, and she told me to get lost. You're the nicest, that's for sure! Lindsey's nice, too, but not as nice as you. No one's as nice as you, Holly. . . . She wouldn't dansh with me either!"

"That's because you're sloshed. You know I'm the

22

only one who loves you enough to dance with you when you're sloshed. Now just hush and try not to embarrass me," she teased.

He began to whine. "You don't really love me, Holly. We used to be so in love, you and me, when we used to date each other. . . ."

She interrupted him, exasperated. Every time he drank, it was the same thing—over and over. "I *do* love you, Billy. You and Lindsey are my best friends, and you know it! But we *never* dated, and I wish you'd quit saying we did!"

He waved a scolding finger in her face. "That's not true! You did *too* go out with me! My mom drove us, and we went to the petting zoo. She packed us a sack lunch: peanut butter and jellies, apple juice and Hostess Twinkies. I spent my whole allowance buying nuts for you to feed the goats—twenty-five whole cents! Then that stupid goat ate a hole in my Gumby shirt!"

Holly laughed. "That was in *third* grade!"

"Yeah. Those were the good old days, weren't they, Hol?"

"For sure," she teased.

"Will you go shopping with me after school on Friday, just for a while?"

"What for?"

"I gotta buy a toy or somethin'."

"For who?"

"Just for . . . someone. Will you come or not?"

"Sure."

Jeff and Cindy were next to them now on the dance floor. Holly and Lindsey giggled at each other as they stared over the shoulders of their dancing partners and gawked at Jeff's tall, handsome body. He held Cindy close and seemed to float across the dance floor—unlike Billy, who staggered back and forth, ready to fall. Holly was using all the strength she had to hold him up.

"I think I've had enough danshing for now, Billy Boy. Let's go sit down."

"Not 'til the music's over," he protested. He tripped over his own feet. "Sorry."

When Jeff saw Billy stumble, he flashed a smile at Holly and gave her a wink.

She thought she'd *die!* Jeff Reynolds actually raised his eyebrows and smiled at her! She struggled to hold Billy up, until he lost his balance and crashed into Doug Jetty, who was standing with his back to the dancers. The impact startled Doug. He wheeled around, his huge fist clenched tightly and aimed right at Billy's nose.

Jeff saw the whole thing and grabbed Billy by the shoulder, pulling him out of Doug's reach. "Hey, little buddy, you gonna make it?" He turned to Doug, "He didn't mean anything," Jeff apologized. "He just lost his balance."

Doug's chest was heaving. His nostrils flared, reminding Holly of an angry bull ready to charge.

"Well, he better be more careful unless he wants his nose broke!" Doug said.

"Yeah, sure."

Almost everyone had stopped dancing. They all watched as Jeff stood coolly and confidently, nose to nose with Doug Jetty—the meanest, most hateful tackle on the Kennedy High football team and, possibly, in the whole world.

Lindsey and Holly stared at each other, feeling

24

proud—and a little surprised—that Jeff had taken their side and stood up for their friend. After all, they were *only* sophomores.

"Jeff, he's drunk! Just leave him alone," Cindy whined.

"I can see that he's drunk, Cindy. I just don't want him crashing to the floor, that's all."

"Thanks," Holly said, helping Billy to the table. "I'll take care of him."

"I hope he's not driving you home," Jeff said.

"No, I walked over."

"Well, at least let me get him into a chair."

Cindy was visibly annoyed. "While you're playing nursemaid, I'm going to the ladies' room." She walked away in a huff.

"Kevin, take Billy outside, will you?" Holly asked. "He needs some fresh air."

"I'll take him," Jeff offered.

"He's my friend. I can take him," Holly said.

"That's okay, I don't mind." Jeff put an arm around Billy and helped him toward the door.

Cindy was in front of the mirror, fixing her makeup.

Holly was sure that once she got to know her, she would find out that all the stories had been greatly exaggerated.

"I like your outfit," Holly said.

Cindy didn't bother to thank her for the compliment. "I take pride in my appearance," she said without taking her eyes off her own reflection.

She put the top back on her lipstick and looked at

Holly. "Do I know you?" she asked coldly.

"I'm Holly Henderson. We met last summer at Cheer Camp. I'm on the sophomore squad."

"Oh," she said, looking at Holly's outfit, "that's nice."

"We have study hall together, third hour," Holly added enthusiastically.

Cindy knew they had study hall together, and she knew Holly was on the cheer squad, though she pretended she didn't.

Holly waited for a response. When there was none, she continued anyway: "Well, there must be over fifty kids in that hall. I can see how you wouldn't notice me."

Cindy smiled wryly. "Oh, I've noticed you, all right. *Everyone* notices you!"

Holly squinted. "That wasn't a compliment, was it?"

"No offense intended . . . Holly, was it?" She dabbed blush on her cheeks.

"Yes. 'Holly,' like in 'jolly.'"

"Well, Holly-like-in-jolly, it's just that you wear those kooky outfits all the time so it's sort of hard to miss you. Tell me, are you one of those 'thrift' shoppers? You know, the ones who like to pick over the racks at the Salvation Army?"

"I like thrift shopping. The clothes have more character," Holly said, not allowing the remark to upset her.

"Somehow, I knew you were going to say that," Cindy said sarcastically. Then she added, "I saw you and your little friend looking at Jeff."

Holly raised her hand. "Guilty!" she admitted with a meek smile.

Cindy's eyes narrowed as she spat words in Holly's face. "Jeff's *mine*! Don't even *think* about him, or I'll ruin you!"

It felt like a slap across the face. Holly's first inclination was to defend herself, but against what? She hadn't done anything!

"Excuse me." Cindy pushed her out of the way as she put one hand on the door.

"Wait a minute," Holly said. "I almost forgot why I came in here. Brenda said she's got something really important to tell you and you're supposed to wait for her here."

"Oh?"

"Yeah. She said she'll be a few minutes, but not to worry. Just wait until she comes."

"Well, I hope she's not too long. . . ."

Billy sat on the curb in the parking lot of The Fantastic, his head between his knees. "I feel like when I was a kid on the merry-go-round. My ma used to push me 'til I was spinnin' so fast I thought I'd fly off into space."

"A little dizzy, huh?" Jeff didn't really sound very sympathetic.

"More than a little."

"Why do you drink so much? Every time I see you you're like this. Aren't you the one who was passed out in the john on Friday?" He didn't wait for an answer because he knew for sure that this was the same kid. "What's your name, anyway?"

"Billy. Bill."

"Well, listen, Billy Bill. It's not too cool to drink yourself into oblivion all the time. Someday you're gonna bump into someone like Doug in there, and you're gonna get hurt. Besides, why would anyone with a pretty girl like you've got wanna get so drunk that he can't even dance with her?"

Billy lifted his head. "Who? You mean Holly?" he asked groggily. "Oh, yeah, she's pretty and nice, too. She's so nice. But she's not my girlfriend."

"She's not? Whose girlfriend is she?"

"She's everyone's friend. Everyone likes Holly."

"But who does *Holly* like? Does she go with anyone?"

"No. I guess not."

Jeff smiled. "Hmmm. . . . Okay. Now, let's get you back inside. I'm gonna keep an eye on you until you sober up. You're not driving, are you?"

"No."

"Good."

When Holly got back to the dance floor, Jeff was helping Billy into a chair. Kevin was forcing him to drink a soda, thinking the caffeine in the cola might sober him up.

"How's he doing?" Holly asked.

"He'll make it," Jeff said. "Who'd he come with?"

"Marty."

"Which one's Marty?"

"The one in the plaid shirt."

"Oh, great! He's no better off than this one! Don't you know anyone who stays sober?" he kidded. Then seriously, he said, "I hope you don't let your friends get behind the wheel of a car when they get like this."

"No. Someone always keeps the car keys," she said honestly.

"Good. People I know are out on the street. The last thing I want is for one of them to be killed by a drunk driver!"

Sandy sat across the table, ogling Jeff and straining to hear his words over the music.

"You guys drink too much," Jeff accused. "It's not cool."

Kevin felt like he should defend his friends—and himself. He was tempted to tell Jeff to mind his own business, but he didn't because there was no meanness or contempt in Jeff's voice. There was only concern.

"Billy just likes to have a good time," Kevin said.

"Right, he looks like he's having a *great* time. I've seen mashed potatoes with more color!"

Billy's head rested heavily on the table. He felt as if it would explode if he tried to lift it.

"You guys better be careful," Jeff cautioned.

He turned to Holly. "You wanna dance?"

She looked around, not sure that he was talking to her.

"Yes!" she said.

He took her hand and led her onto the dance floor. "I like your earrings." He touched the tiny wooden fruit that dangled loosely from the hooked wire. "Makes me crave fruit salad," he teased.

"I thought they made a real fashion statement." Then Holly felt the fluttering of a thousand tiny butterflies as Jeff put his arm around her, and they began to dance. He looked directly into her eyes. "So how's

29

everything on the sophomore cheer squad?"

"How'd you know I was on the cheer squad?"

He winked at her. "Girls like you don't get missed. You're Holly Henderson, right?"

"Yes."

He held out his hand in greeting. "I'm Jeff Reynolds."

He said his name just like he was an ordinary person. It was as if he didn't even know he was the most popular boy in school.

Holly shook his hand, hopeful he wouldn't feel the nervous perspiration on her palm. She'd imagined this moment for a year and a half, and now it was actually happening.

She stared at the blue wool of his letterman's sweater when she spoke: "How's things on the football team? Well, actually I know how things are because the cheer squad goes to every game. . . . I'm just a little nervous. Did you know there was a bearded baby born once? Oh gosh, I bet that sounded really stupid, didn't it?" She looked around nervously. "Where's Lindsey?"

"*Who's* Lindsey?" he asked, amused by her jitters.

"She's my best friend. We walked over together, and if she leaves without me, I'll have to walk home alone. I hate that. . . . My mom hates it too because she always thinks some awful, horrible fate awaits me. What time is it?" She rambled like an endless country road, appearing to go nowhere.

When Holly finally looked at him, he was smiling down at her. His smile was so warm she thought she'd melt right into her new shoes. She pictured Jeff, standing on the dance floor, staring down at a pair of red

30

shoes, ruined with the runny, melted remains of Holly Henderson.

"You're nice," he said softly.

"You're the most gorgeous person I've ever seen!" She blurted the words out before she could stop herself. Then she felt her face turn red with embarrassment. Both her hands covered her mouth as if even more stupid remarks were waiting, anxious to escape. "Oh . . . I can't believe I said that!"

"Why not?" he laughed. "My mom says it almost every day!"

The music had stopped, and they stood on the dance floor, looking into each other's eyes. Lindsey was passing by, and Holly caught a glimpse of her. Her mouth dropped open when she heard Jeff ask Holly to dance with him again.

She stared with envy as they moved gracefully on the dance floor, so mesmerized that she barely noticed Cindy standing beside her, breathing heavily.

"That little *witch*!" Cindy said. "Brenda, my fanny!"

Lindsey turned to her. "I think they make a lovely couple," she said and walked away.

CHAPTER THREE

Holly opened the front door, surprised to see her mother sitting in the large wing-backed chair in front of the fireplace. The grandfather clock read 11:15.

"Hi, Mom. You're home early," she said, only a little flustered.

"Yes, I am. And you're home late! Where have you been?"

"I went to The Fantastic with Lindsey."

"When you have *school* tomorrow?" She said "school" with horror in her voice—as if she'd said, "When you have *brain surgery* tomorrow?"

Her mother continued, "When you called me at the station you said you were going to study!"

"Mom, it's Wednesday night. Girls get in free, and *everyone* goes on Wednesday night!"

"Everyone but you! Your grades have been slipping miserably, Holly. The last thing you need is to be out *dancing* on a school night!"

"I know, Mom, but I get so lonely sitting here night

33

after night all by myself. There's no one to talk to. I *hate* being alone!"

"Holly, I'm working evenings in addition to my regular job. Even though my situation at the station is only temporary, I'm under a tremendous amount of stress right now. I don't think it's fair that I should have to come home and deal with this!

"I know this change is difficult for you, but you're sixteen years old. It's not as though you were ten or eleven. The last thing I need is for you to add to my stress by breaking all the rules. You've done this before, haven't you?"

"Yes."

"How many times?"

Holly was annoyed now. "I don't know! What difference does it make?"

"It makes a lot of difference. You've been lying to me! You lied to me tonight, too! You told me you were going to study. Is this why your grades have been slipping so badly? Are you going out every night when you're supposed to be home studying?"

"Mom, I don't go out every single night!"

Carol Henderson got up and began pacing the room. Holly could feel a lecture coming on, and her mother didn't disappoint her. "Holly, not only is it too late to be out on a school night, but when you leave the house and don't tell me where you're going, *anything* could happen to you, and I'd never know it! There are kids abducted and molested—even *murdered*—every day because they do silly things like sneaking out of the house at night! Don't you think about what could happen when you do things like this?"

"Oh, gimme a break, Mom! You act like I was hitch-hiking up to Haight-Ashbury or something! I only went a couple of blocks! And it isn't like I was alone—Lindsey was with me. . . ."

"That's not the point! I thought we trusted each other. I thought you understood the rules. It's danger-ous out there. Any number of things can happen!" She pointed out the front window, as if there were a serial killer on the porch. "We have rules for *reasons*, Holly, and I expect you to follow them!"

"I'm sorry!"

Her mother paced back to her chair and sat down. She crossed one leg over the other and jiggled her foot nervously. "Well, what do you think we should do about this?"

As a psychologist, Carol Henderson thought it pru-dent to allow Holly to choose her own punishments. When Holly was younger, she considered this a privi-lege; it made her feel grown up and in control of her own destiny. But after a while, it became an added pressure. She wished that just *once* in her life her parents would make a decision for her.

The whole thing was a sham anyway as far as Holly was concerned. Her parents went through the motions of having rules, but lately, they didn't take the time or make the effort to enforce them.

"I don't know. *You're* the mother. You tell me."

"It's good for you to think this out for yourself, Holly. After all, *you* committed the crime."

"Crime? Mom, sneaking out of the house isn't a crime! *Murder* is a crime. *Grand theft auto* is a crime. Sneaking out at night is just something kids do for *fun*!"

"Is that all you can think about—*fun*? This is *life*, Holly, and life is a responsibility! You have a *responsibility* to do your school work. You have a *responsibility* to me. You're not getting things done around the house, and you're breaking the rules! I don't need your definition of 'crime,' Holly. And if you think worrying your mother to death is 'fun,' I'd say you have a warped sense of humor and you should study the definition of *that*!"

Holly shook her finger playfully at her mother, attempting to make light of the conversation. "You know, you're not the first person who's accused me of being warped!" She jumped on the couch and laid down, folding her hands across her chest. Then in her best German accent she said, "Tell me, Doctor Hen-n-derson, vot do you zink is vrong vis me? Do you zink I am *clrazy*?"

"Holly, it's not funny! Now what do you think is a fair punishment for what you did?"

"How about death by lethal injection?"

"That's not funny, either!"

"Well, I don't know! How about grounding?"

"That's a good one."

Holly knew it was a good one because it never worked. Her mom and dad were never home, so there was no possible way she ever stayed grounded. She played along anyway. "Okay, I'll take grounding. What do you think is fair? How long, I mean?"

"You tell me."

"How about . . . two weekends, since I'm not allowed out on school nights anyway?"

"That's fair."

"Okay, I'm officially grounding myself for two

36

weekends. Now, Mom, you'll never guess what happened at The Fantastic! There's this boy, Jeff. . . ."

Her mother stopped her in mid-sentence with a big yawn. She got up and kissed Holly on the cheek. "Honey, I'd love to hear about it in the morning. Right now, I'm just too tired. I'm still not used to working two jobs.

"I'm glad you got home safely. And I'm glad you had a great time—even though you disobeyed me. But I've *gotta* get some sleep. I have a 7:30 appointment in the morning. You go right to bed. It's late."

Holly watched her mother disappear up the stairs. She wouldn't have time to listen to her in the morning, either. She'd be too hurried, afraid that she might keep a patient waiting. The ticking of the old grandfather clock made Holly lonesome for Grandma Rachel. The old oak clock was the only thing left of hers, and Holly seldom heard it chime without thinking of her grandma. Oh, she missed her Grandma Rachel so much. Grandma was never too tired to listen to her. . . .

The clock said 11:35, but Holly wasn't tired. She wondered if her mom would tell her dad that she'd sneaked out. After closer consideration, she figured that her dad probably would never find out. He was seldom home, and when he was, his conversations with his wife were about much more important things than Holly: finances, social engagements, and the problems they both faced in their successful—but stressful—careers.

The forlorn ticking of the clock depressed her. After a while, she went to the stairway and walked up a few steps until she could see the door to her mother's room.

There was no light coming from under it, so she was certain her mother was in bed.

Holly crept back to the living room and went to the bar. Taking some ice cubes from the freezer below, she quietly put them in a glass and filled it half full with vodka. Then she sank back into her chair and took a long swallow . . . just to relax so she could sleep.

❖ ❖ ❖

The bell sounded for lunch and all the classroom doors opened at once, spilling excited kids, like BB's from a box, into the hallways and stairwells of Kennedy High. Shouting voices echoed commands: "Meet in the quad for lunch!" "Gimme back my book, you jerk!" "Quit shoving!" Locker doors slammed and whistles sent piercing screams down the hallways as teachers warned students not to run.

"This place is a *zoo!*" Holly said.

Lindsey was more interested in the latest gossip. "So, what happened last period in study hall? Did she say anything?"

"Who?"

"Cindy, dummy!"

"No. She didn't say anything. What did you think she'd say?"

"Well, honestly, Holly, what would *you* say? You practically *stole* her boyfriend right out from under her snotty little nose! Everyone in the whole school's talking about it. You made a total *fool* out of her!"

Holly stopped, facing her friend directly. "Is that what you think?"

"That's what everyone thinks! Do you know how

many kids in this school would have given a year's free pass to the movies just to make Cindy Aldrich look like a fool? And *you* did it—without even trying! You're a legend, Holly, a *legend!* The kids are talking about dedicating a fountain in your honor."

"That's silly. I never meant to make a fool out of anyone. I just wanted to dance with Jeff." Her eyes grew dreamy. "Isn't he *gorgeous?* Here, hold these, will you?" She handed Lindsey her books.

Now that Lindsey was laden with books and totally helpless, Holly began rummaging through the large bookbag that dangled loosely from her friend's arm. She dug through everything until she found the rumpled lunch sack. Victoriously, she pulled it out.

"Not again, Holly!" Lindsey protested. "I can't believe you got me again!"

Holly was looking inside the wrinkled bag. "It's *roast beef,*" she almost shouted. "Oh, Lins, this is great!"

"Holly, you're *not* taking my roast beef sandwich! I love roast beef!" she whined.

"Oh come on, Lins! You can have roast beef any time. You know my mom never cooks! Please?"

Lindsey thought a moment. "What're they having in the cafeteria?"

"Let's see . . . it's Thursday . . . *pizza!*"

"I hate the pizza here. It tastes like grease on a bagel!"

"Oh, it's not so bad. We'll split. I'll give you one piece of pizza and you give me half of your sandwich. That's a good deal, isn't it?"

"Okay," Lindsey agreed reluctantly.

They took their food outside and ate in their usual

39

spot. There was no "Reserved" sign, but everyone knew where Holly and Lindsey could be found at lunchtime. Their table was in the corner closest to the snack bar and was shaded by a huge tree of some unknown species. The only reason they got that table was because the bird droppings were a problem. Otherwise, it would have been taken by upperclassmen because it was such a choice location. Everyone who used the snack bar had to walk past their table.

They had just sat down to eat when Lindsey noticed a group of senior boys walking toward the snack bar. She threw her pizza on the table, turning her face away from them and covering her eyes. "Oh my gosh," she said, "here he comes!"

Unfazed by her dramatics, Holly simply said, "Here *who* comes?"

"Jeff, you goofball!"

Holly looked up, wiping the pizza sauce from her mouth with the back of her hand. There were five jocks walking together, talking and laughing loudly at something Jeff was saying. "Would you just relax? He's not coming over here. He's just walking to the snack bar!"

They watched intently as the boys came closer, until finally, they were right in front of the girls' table. Jeff looked right at Holly, seeming not to notice her as he talked. Then he turned, right in the middle of a sentence, and walked over to her. "Hi! How's the dancin' queen?"

She tried to maintain her composure. She tried to act as if this were a common occurrence. "Fine, thank you."

"You going back to The Fantastic tonight?"

"Yeah. Are you?"

"Yeah. I'll see you there. Well, gotta go."

Lindsey moved up and down in her seat, like a five-year-old in need of a trip to the bathroom. Her hands were clasped tightly in her lap as she moved excitedly, trying in vain to contain herself. "I don't believe this is happening! I simply don't believe this! He almost asked you out!"

"Oh, Lins, come on. He just asked if I was going to The Fantastic. That's hardly like asking me for a date!"

"How can you say that? How can you act so casual? Do you know what this means? He must like you, mallet head!"

"Oh my *gosh*! Do you really think so?" Holly covered her mouth with her hands to keep herself from screaming out loud.

They watched, dumbstruck, as Jeff stood in line, got his food, and came back past their table in search of a place to sit. Holly was trying to act indifferent, but she was watching his every move out of the corner of her eye.

"Anyone sitting here?" he asked, climbing over the bench to sit opposite Holly.

"No," she said, resisting the thought that she would probably die of excitement before lunch was over.

Jeff's friend Ryan sat down next to him and the two began discussing the upcoming football game.

Lindsey grabbed Holly's leg under the table, squeezing her knee until Holly almost cried out in pain. No words were necessary, Holly knew what she was thinking: *Here they were, low-life sophomores, sharing*

41

a table with the two most popular, handsome boys in school!

Out of the corner of her eye, Holly saw Melissa, Jennifer, and Sandy across the quad, giggling wildly and pointing at them. Sandy took a piece of paper and a large marker from her notebook and began scribbling. When she showed the paper to her friends, they laughed out loud. When Jeff turned to see what all the noise was about, the girls pretended innocence.

"Are those friends of yours?" he asked, turning back toward Holly.

"Yeah. They're a little *immature*," she said, shouting the word *immature*.

In response, Sandy smiled and, with Jeff's back to her, held the sign up for Holly to see:

CINDY: 0
HOLLY: 2

❖ ❖ ❖

Kids hung around Holly like ants on a picnic basket. Her locker was *the* meeting place between classes and after school. Today was no different, but instead of the usual kidding and idle conversation, the girls wanted to hear every last detail of the night before at The Fantastic. Lindsey did all the talking as Holly searched the awful mess that was her locker for Billy's history book.

"It's gotta be in there," he was saying over Lindsey's excited narrative. "I know I put it in there 'cause I couldn't remember my combination."

Finally she found it and gave it to him, annoyed that he had made *his* history book *her* problem. "You know, Billy, it's almost two months into the school year. I'd think you could remember your combination by now."

He smiled dumbly. She went to shut the locker, but his hand stopped her. "Ah . . . I left somethin' else in there, too." He dug through the books, pom-poms, and dirty gym clothes until he found a small brown bag.

"Ah-h-h," he said, covering the bag with several little kisses. "Come to Daddy." He looked around cautiously before he removed the pint-sized bottle from the bag. "Wanna swig?" he offered.

"No thanks. I never drink before five o'clock."

"It's five o'clock someplace!" he cracked, taking a long drink. He held it out to her again. "Go ahead!"

She looked at him wearily. "You're hopeless!"

When Lindsey saw the bottle, she almost shouted her warning: "Billy! Put that away! What're you trying to do, get yourself *expelled*? Honestly, Billy, you're acting crazy with that stuff lately. You gotta be more careful!" She wondered about Billy's carelessness. It was as if he didn't care about anything anymore.

He tucked the bottle under his jacket and started toward the parking lot, yelling to Holly over his shoulder: "Don't forget about tomorrow after school. You promised to go shopping with me!"

"So anyway," Lindsey continued to the girls, "Cindy sat in the bathroom for about half an hour waiting for Brenda, and of course, she never showed up. . . ."

"It wasn't a half hour, Lindsey," Holly corrected, "it was more like ten minutes."

"Ten minutes . . . half an hour. What's the difference? The fact is, you got her *good!*"

A huge smile crossed Holly's lips. "Yeah. I did,

43

didn't I?" They all laughed. "Well, listen, guys, we gotta go to cheer practice. Lindsey, are you ready?"

She quickly gathered up her pom-poms and gym shoes as Holly attempted to hurry Sandy along. "Come on, Sands! We gotta fly. If I'm late again, Miss Connors will kick me off the squad."

"Fat chance," Sandy said, talking to the others. "Holly could stand on her head naked with her tongue hanging out, and Miss Connors wouldn't bat an eye! Now on the other hand, if I dropped dead, she'd get ticked off because I fell the wrong way!"

"I think you're exaggerating . . . but only slightly," Holly kidded.

"Everyone knows you're Miss Connors' pet. In fact, you're *every* teacher's pet!"

"Miss Connors is only nice to me because she's in love with my dad. She hasn't missed an episode of *Sutton Street* in eight years. Why do you think she takes her lunch hour at ten o'clock?"

"Well, that may have *something* to do with it, but she always makes *me* do extra workout!" Sandy whined.

Holly puckered her lips and teased Sandy in baby talk: "Oh, poor widow baby! Does the mean owd teacher pick on widow Sandy-kins?"

Sandy hit Holly playfully over the head with her pom-poms and chased her down the hall toward the gym.

The other girls were already in line when they got there. Miss Connors blew her whistle, signaling to stop the recording of "On Wisconsin." She shouted to Sandy, "Miss Yates, you're *late!*"

Sandy gave Holly an "I told you so" look, and the three girls took their places in the cheer line as the music started up again.

Looking more like a drill instructor than a cheerleading coach, Miss Connors stood stiffly, legs apart, hands on her hips, watching the girls dance. Every once in a while she'd clap her hands to the music and shout "Get those legs up. Higher. *Higher!* Watch the girl next to you. . . . Smile! That's great, Holly. . . . Everyone look at Holly!"

All of a sudden, Holly crashed to the floor, her right leg folding under her. Miss Connors blew her whistle hysterically as the other girls crowded around.

"What happened?"

"Are you all right?"

Miss Connors waved her arms wildly. "Don't walk all over her, for Pete's sake! Give her some air!" She bent over, her big bosom nearly smothering Holly. "What happened?"

Holly scrunched up her face as she massaged her leg. "I don't know. . . . I was doing fine when my leg just sort of gave out on me."

"Try to unbend it."

She stretched her leg out slowly, screwing her face up in pain. "I . . . it hurts really bad!"

"Lindsey, help Holly to the locker room and put some ice on her leg."

Lindsey's voice oozed sympathy as she bent down to help Holly up. "Easy now. I won't hurt you. Just put all your weight on my shoulder. . . . We'll go real slow. Be careful, now."

Straining visibly, Holly draped her arm around

45

Lindsey's shoulder and pulled herself up. She moved slowly, wincing as she was forced to put weight on her leg. She smiled weakly as the girls applauded, signaling how much they appreciated her bravery.

"Don't put too much weight on it!" Miss Connors warned. "Oh dear. Oh dear, *oh dear!* This is all we need. Cheer competition only six weeks away and my *best dancer* down!"

Sandy tried to comfort her, certain some sympathy would put her in better favor with the teacher. "Don't worry, Miss Connors, Holly'll be all right. She's tough as nails!"

"I hope you're right. If we lose Holly now, we may as well kiss that trophy *and* the trip to Las Vegas goodbye!"

When they got to the locker room, Lindsey cautioned her friend again. "The floor's slippery. Don't walk too fast."

Holly sank onto the bench in front of her locker. Lindsey sat next to her, deeply concerned about her friend's suffering. "Gosh, this is awful! Does it really hurt?"

Holly only winced, massaging the leg.

"Keep it elevated when you get home tonight, and you can't walk on it at all."

"Okay," Holly said weakly. "But can I do this?" She jumped off the bench and began dancing crazily around the locker room. She leaped up and down, did spins and turned cartwheels until she crashed into the lockers, banging her head against the cold steel. "Ouch!"

"It serves you right!" Lindsey said, pretending anger. "You little *faker!* Why'd you do that?"

46

"Because *we* are going to The Fantastic tonight, and *we* have to shop for new outfits!"

"We can't do that! What if someone sees you at the mall?"

"We won't go to *our* mall, mallet head! We'll ride the bus over to Eastland Mall."

"Oh, yeah . . . we could do that."

"Then let's do it!"

Holly heard footsteps running into the locker room and sat down quickly, stretching her leg out in front of her.

"How is it, dear?" Miss Connors asked.

Holly rubbed her leg. "It *really* hurts."

Miss Connors looked at her skeptically. "I thought it was the other leg?"

Holly shot a quick glance at Lindsey, who bailed her out in great style. "Oh, no, Miss Connors, it was her left leg, all right. I remember."

Lindsey knelt and began feeling the leg as if she had a degree from Harvard Medical School. "There doesn't seem to be any swelling, but she should really stay off it and have a doctor check it. She may have a bone chip or something!"

Miss Connors was truly fretful. "Oh dear, oh dear! I think you'd better go home and call your family doctor. Can someone come and pick you up?"

"No, my mom works and my dad's out of town."

Miss Connors' eyes grew dreamy as she recalled the shot of Beau Collins in the moonlight on *Sutton Street* the day before.

"Oh," she said, not quite back to reality, ". . . that was some shock when Trish got pushed off the balcony,

47

wasn't it? Well, I can't say I'm surprised. You know what they say: You play, you pay. Who do you think did it?"

"I think it was Tanya. I think Beau's the father of Tanya's baby so she killed Trish so she could have Beau all for herself."

Miss Connors contemplated Holly's theory.

"Well, listen," Lindsey said nervously, "I've got my bike so I'll ride Holly home."

"That will be fine. But *be careful!* When you get home, be sure to elevate that leg. Keep ice on it for at least fifteen minutes every hour. And don't forget to call your doctor!"

"Yes, Miss Connors."

CHAPTER FOUR

"**I** love you!" the voice on the telephone said.

"I love you, too, Daddy!"

"Did you watch the show today?"

"Not yet. Lindsey and I went shopping. I got. . . ."

"Whaddaya mean 'not yet'? You're the only fan I have left! If you don't watch, who will?"

She made her voice sing-songy. "Miss-ss Con-nors will!"

"I'm serious, you little bugger! Why didn't you watch?"

"I told you I went shopping! I'll watch it later, I promise. Daddy, I met this great guy. . . ."

"They cut my lines again," he complained.

"How bad?"

"Really bad. I know they're trying to write me out. . . . They wanna make room for a younger guy, I'm sure of it."

"No way! That show would roll over and *die* without Beau! They won't write you out. Hey, Daddy, I . . . ."

His voice grew anxious, "I don't know, Hol. I'm

getting older. I don't look as good as I did. There's always someone waiting in the wings to take my job."

"Oh, Daddy, lighten up! You're only forty-three."

"Forty!" he corrected.

"You're forty-three, and you know it! Anyway, what difference does age make? You're devastatingly handsome. Miss Connors would give up tea with Princess Di and Fergie just to have your autograph!"

Holly was balancing the phone on her shoulder, rummaging through her dressing table drawers for the perfect necklace to go with her new outfit.

"What do you think of Johnny Willows?"

"The actor?" Clearly, she wasn't concentrating on the question. Where was her silver necklace?

"No, Johnny Willows the trained monkey. Yes, the actor!"

"He's fabulous looking," she said honestly.

"Oh, that's encouraging!"

She tried to stay interested in the conversation, but she was anxious to get to The Fantastic.

"Daddy, you worry too much. Everything'll be all right. Hey, Daddy, I'm in a little bit of a hurry."

"Well, I'll let you go then. Tell Mom I'll call her at the office tommorrow."

Holly finished dressing, frustrated as usual by the call. Every time she tried to share something with her father, he made her feel as if her news were secondary to his problems. He always worried that someone was going to take his job. And he needed constant reassurance that he was good looking, as if his acting ability had nothing to do with his success. More often than not, when T. J. Henderson called his daughter, it was

50

because he wanted some moral support.

Holly thought that daughters should go to their fathers with their problems, not the other way around.

❖ ❖ ❖

T. J. Henderson remained by the phone, upset with himself for forgetting to ask his daughter about her science project. He knew she was having difficulty with it, and he'd promised to give her some help. He'd forgotten all about it once he got home last weekend. It seemed that he just couldn't keep his mind on anything lately.

Exhausted, he fell back on the bed, closed his eyes, and massaged his forehead. This had been the worst week of his life.

He rolled over and picked up his copy of *Variety*. The theatrical newspaper was open to the "Soap" section. The worrisome headline loomed before him: "Johnny Willow to Get Lead Status on *Sutton Street*."

The article said Johnny Willow's character, Vance Howard, was going to take over the role of leading man. If that happened, T. J.'s character, Beau Collins, would either be killed off or reduced to smaller and smaller parts, until finally, he was off the show altogether. Either way, the end result would be the same: T. J. Henderson would be out of a job.

He tossed the paper on the floor. For six weeks there had been speculation about his position on the show, but the producers never said anything directly to him. All he knew was what he read in *Variety* or *TV Guide*.

Not knowing seemed cruel and unusual punishment

to him. He wished they'd just fire him if that's what they were going to do. At least it would be over quickly. This was like a slow, agonizing death. He felt constant anxiety, not knowing from one day to the next whether he had a job or not.

If they *did* fire him, he felt it would be impossible to get a job with the same status as that of Beau Collins. Jobs like his were few and far between. At the age of forty-three, there was the painful reality that he may be considered too old to play a leading role. He sighed deeply, imagining his career as over, his livelihood plucked from him like a feather from a chicken.

He walked to the mirror and surveyed himself carefully. Pushing the thick, black hair off his forehead, he noticed he was getting grayer there and around his temples. He studied the deep creases in his forehead and the lines around his eyes. Turning this way and that, he observed himself from different angles. The lines, he decided, were mother nature's roadmap to the land of old age and unemployment.

He climbed into bed and turned out the light, feeling lonely and depressed. He was certain that if Carol were there, she would diagnose his condition as "midlife crisis."

It seemed only yesterday that he was a student at UCLA, taking tickets after classes at the famous Chinese theater in the hope of catching a glimpse of someone famous. Merely starstruck, it had never occurred to him to attempt acting himself.

Then one day, T. J.'s friend invited him to go to a product testing.

"Just show up," his friend said. "Try the product.

They'll ask you what you think of it, and they'll pay you fifteen dollars. It's that simple."

Eager to get the fifteen dollars so he could take Carol to the stage production of *Grease,* T. J. went to the testing.

A long table had been set up in an otherwise empty hotel room. It was covered by a white tablecloth, and there were six cereal bowls with spoons spaced evenly in front of chairs along one side. On the other side of the table, a man in a business suit sat opposite each bowl. Behind the men was a large mirror. T. J.'s friend told him there was a camera behind the mirror and the whole test was being filmed.

The product they were testing was Berry Oats cereal. Coincidentally, it had been T. J.'s absolute favorite since he was a little boy.

He had skipped breakfast that day in order to get to the test on time, and now he was starving. He dug into the cereal hungrily, unaware of the businessman's delight.

"You like that cereal?" the businessman asked.

With his mouth full, and his spoon aimed back at the bowl, T. J. answered, "Are you kiddin'? This is the *greatest* stuff! I've been eatin' this stuff since I was a little kid. I love it!"

The man laughed. "Would you say Berry Oats made you what you are today?"

T. J. laughed back. "What? Flunking physics? No, Berry Oats isn't responsible for that, but it's great stuff!"

Excitedly, the man jumped up from the table, yelling, "Cut! Cut! This is perfect!"

Startled, T. J. stood up. "What's wrong?"

"Wrong?" the man said. "Nothing's wrong. Everything's right. You're perfect for the part!"

"Part? What part?"

"The commercial!"

"What commerical?"

"The one we're taping right now. You mean you didn't know?"

"I knew you were filming me, but I didn't know it was for a commercial!"

"Well, it is, and you got the part. Rubin! Get this kid a contract!"

That commercial led to several others, some guest spots on national television shows, and eventually, his job on *Sutton Street*.

T. J. judged himself a success. He made a better-than-average salary, and for the most part, he liked what he was doing to earn it. But it had never been easy. Hollywood chewed up people like him and spit them in the wind.

The job demands were hectic. And there was always someone younger, more attractive, trying to take his job. Every time the ratings fell, someone was going to be fired. And like everyone else in the cast, T. J. thought it would be him next time.

Because knowing the right people was as important as knowing one's lines, T. J.'s social schedule was as hectic as his work schedule. When it became too demanding, he moved his family from California and was forced to suffer the inconvenience of travel each week, just so he could have time alone with his wife and daughter.

He hated the personal appearances: Autograph

signing parties, ladies' luncheons, cocktail parties with people he found obnoxious. The only appearances he enjoyed were the speaking engagements he frequently did for the drama departments at colleges and universities in the area. He liked teaching the kids.

Lying on his bed, thinking back, T. J. found it odd that, in spite of all the drawbacks in his career, he'd never considered doing anything else.

It was almost nine o'clock when they arrived at The Fantastic, because Holly had waited for her mother's "checkup call." She had thought about initiating the call herself so she could leave earlier, but she was afraid her mother might suspect something if she did.

Jeff was standing near the door when she came in. He didn't want to miss her. He greeted her warmly. "Hi!"

"Hi, yourself!"

"Wanna dance?"

She looked at Lindsey for approval. "Don't worry about me. I'm going in search of the perfect man."

"Well, then," Holly said, "I guess it's okay."

She felt awkward trying to shout over the music, so she just danced, avoiding his eyes. When the song was over, he pointed to a table in the corner where Ryan Cummins was sitting. "I saved that table over there. Go sit down while I get us something to drink."

As soon as he came back, Ryan excused himself. "I've got him trained," Jeff joked.

They sipped their Cokes in silence. Finally, he said, "So tell me about yourself."

55

"What do you want me to tell you?"

He scratched his head. After some thought, he asked, "How much did you weigh when you were born?"

"Forty-seven pounds," she said, not hesitating a second.

He laughed. "That must have been painful!"

"Yes, quite. And my mother thinks I'm a pain to this day!"

He leaned across the table and said, "Okay, goofy, I'm serious here. Tell me something about yourself."

"Okay, Pluto, here goes: My name is Holly Rachel Henderson. I'm sixteen years old, and my birthday is the fourth of July—just like George M. Cohan and George Steinbrenner, owner of the New York Yankees, though neither of these Georges ever sent me a birthday card.

"I have no brothers or sisters because both of my parents are more career-oriented than kid-oriented. I have no pets because my father has asthma.

"My mother's a psychologist and has a show on talk radio. She's filling in for someone else, but if her ratings stay up, they may give her her own show. If that happens, I will apply for permanent status as an orphan because I never see her. If you listen to WTLK, you know her as Dr. Carol. . . ."

"I know who she is!" Jeff said excitedly. "Is she really your mother?"

"Really and truly, and she has the stretch marks to prove it. Do you know how *big* a forty-seven-pound baby is?"

He laughed. "You're nuts! Tell me some more."

She sipped her Coke. "Well, if you were impressed by my mother, you'll love this: My father's an actor. He's Beau Collins on *Sutton Street*."

"*No way!* My mom *loves* that show!"

"Well, he's my dad. I don't see him much because he works in Hollywood all week and just comes home for the weekends."

"That's fantastic! But what about *you*? What do *you* do?"

"I like thrift shopping, and I adore old movies. *Really old* movies, with Humphrey Bogart and Lauren Bacall . . . and Bette Davis! She's my absolute favorite."

"I don't think I've ever watched one of those movies all the way through."

"Oh, you should! They're great. The dialogue's really good, but you have to pay close attention because they talk so fast."

He was staring over her shoulder toward the door and his expression told her something was wrong. She looked around and saw Cindy standing in the doorway with Doug Jetty.

There was a rivalry between Jeff and Doug that had gone on since their freshman year and everyone in school knew about it. It was perfectly clear to Holly—and Jeff too—that Cindy had shown up with Doug in an effort to make Jeff jealous. Holly started to get up. "I don't want to start anything. . . . I'll just go find Lindsey."

He grabbed her hand and pulled her back down. "Oh no you don't! You haven't finished telling me about yourself yet!"

She looked at the door nervously, and her eyes

locked with Cindy's. "I feel really awkward. I think I'd better go."

"Cindy and I broke up," he said bluntly.

"You guys *always* break up!"

"Well, this time we *really* broke up."

"How long have you been going together, anyway?"

"It seems like forever—it *was* forever! I met her in the fourth grade. She was in my Sunday school class. She's really the only girl I've ever dated. Actually," he stirred his drink with his straw, "I *have* broken up with her a lot. But this time it's for good. Except for the homecoming dance . . . she asked me a month ago. I'm serious about breaking up with her, though!"

"Why?"

It was a simple question, but one he hadn't expected. He wanted to tell her the truth about how his life was different now and how he and Cindy just didn't think the same. But he didn't know Holly very well, and he felt somewhat uncomfortable. "I guess we just got tired of each other," he said.

Holly shifted in her chair. "Are you sure *you* broke up with Cindy, or did *she* break up with you?"

"I broke up with her, honest. Why?"

"Well . . . I thought maybe she got mad at you last night."

"She did. But she didn't break up with me. Hey, how'd you know she was mad at me, anyway?"

Holly decided to tell him everything. "I really wanted to dance with you, and I knew you wouldn't ask me if Cindy was with you, so I tricked her into staying in the bathroom. I don't blame you if you're mad. I admit it was a dirty trick. . . ."

58

He smiled widely. "Yeah, it was. Funny, too!" Quickly, he pushed himself away from the table. Still seated, he began tapping his feet erradically to the beat of the music. "I just can't stop these dancing feet!" He jumped up, pulling her behind him.

Cindy and Doug were already on the dance floor. Though it wasn't that crowded, Doug kept bumping into Jeff. Jeff ignored him at first, but Doug started bumping him harder and harder, until finally, he sent Jeff flying into Holly, knocking her to the floor. The other kids stared, a few chuckling at Holly's embarrassment, but most of them stiff from the tension in the room.

By now, Lindsey, Billy, Kevin, and Sandy were right next to Holly, watching with concern as Jeff hurriedly helped her up. "Are you all right?"

She glared at Doug. He was the meanest, ugliest looking person she'd ever seen. There wasn't a single underclassman in the whole school who wasn't afraid of him. His looks were severe enough to intimidate the Boston Strangler: His head was huge and shaved to the scalp. Small, glassy eyes were framed by thick, dark eyebrows. Doug Jetty had a large space between his front teeth and a hideous, raised scar on his chin. And he outweighed Jeff by at least forty pounds. "You did that on purpose!" Holly accused.

Doug pretended innocence, saying nothing.

"I think you just need a more graceful dancing partner, Miss Holly-Jolly," Cindy said. "Why, you look almost as awkward on the dance floor as you do in a cheer line."

Lindsey stepped forward. "You take that back!"

59

Cindy looked at Jeff, as if she expected him to bail her out. When he said nothing, she said to Doug, "Let's go. It's awfully crowded in here."

They turned to leave, but Jeff grabbed Doug by the arm. "Wait a minute! You owe Holly an apology."

Doug stood toe to toe with Jeff, their noses almost touching. "Says *who*?"

Lindsey pushed her way between them. "Says *me*, that's who!" Even *Doug* wouldn't hit a girl, she hoped!

He stared at her, with that awful "I'll crush you" stare that frightened even the toughest opponents on the football field.

Lindsey stared right back, willing to risk life and limb to defend her friend. "What're you gonna do, *punch* me?"

The truth was, he didn't know *what* to do. He'd never been in a position like this before. He couldn't punch her, that was for sure. But he couldn't ignore her either. That would get all over school! He was more than a little flustered.

"Shut up!" he said. "It's none of your business!"

She put her hands on her hips. "I'm *making* it my business! You apologize to her!" she shouted. Then she turned to Cindy: "Tell him to apologize!"

Cindy shifted nervously, concerned about what this would do to her reputation. With homecoming just around the corner, the last thing she needed was to get a bunch of people mad at her . . . their votes could decide whether or not she became queen! She turned to Doug, "We know it was an accident, but maybe you should apologize to. . . . What was your name again?"

"Her name is Holly," Jeff said patiently.

60

"I ain't apologizing to nobody!"

Now it was Jeff's turn. He gently moved Lindsey aside and stood, once again, face to face with the big gorilla. "Look, pal. We know a nice gentleman like you would never purposely shove a lady. We know your gripe's not with Holly. She hasn't done anything to you. So be a good guy and just apologize to her so we can get on with the party."

Doug surveyed the circle of faces. They were all staring at him, waiting. He felt like a total fool. Finally, he apologized, in spite of himself: "I'm sorry. I didn't mean to knock you down."

He took Cindy's hand, and they pushed through the crowd toward the door, with voices mumbling in his ear: "Jerk!" "Big bully!" ". . . shoving Holly like that!"

Doug turned and glared at Jeff. The look in his eyes told everyone that this was not the end of the argument.

CHAPTER FIVE

"I can't be gone too long, Billy. I've got cheer practice at five."

"We'll be back by then."

They walked, hand in hand, the short distance to the mall.

"Are you going to the game tonight?"

"No. I've got other plans."

"What could be more important than watching Kennedy High pound the Wilson Wildcats into the ground?" Holly joked.

He shrugged his shoulders, unwilling to give her an answer. "I've just got stuff to do."

They bought ice cream and sat on stone benches in the center of the mall, laughing at the people going by. They chuckled at mismatched outfits, outrageous hairstyles, and oddly shaped bodies.

They watched mothers with babies and husbands with wives and wondered to each other where all these people had come from and where they might be going.

"See that lady over there?" Billy said, pointing.

Holly saw a rather large lady. Her back was to them as she looked into the window of a pet shop. She wore a red tent-shaped dress that was short enough to show the veins behind her knees. She had on black wing-tipped shoes that could have been her husband's and white sport socks. Her hair was in curlers and covered with a bright, floral-print chiffon scarf.

"Yes, I see her," Holly giggled.

"Well, I happen to know that she owns a pack of pitbulls."

"Is that so?"

"Yes. That's so. Anyway, yesterday she got a mysterious phone call from Waldo Snodgrass—he's a local racketeer—saying that he wants to hire the pitbulls to help him pull a heist. *Tonight*!" He narrowed his eyes and lowered his voice to a sinister whisper. "So, she came here, to *that* pet shop, to purchase a particularly unprincipled poodle named Pierre—a dog with no social conscience at all—to lead the operation."

Holly laughed. "You're goofy!"

"I know. That's why you like me!" He pushed his ice cream cone into her nose.

"Quit it!" she yelled. She dipped her finger in her ice cream and wiped it on his arm. She was trying to get him again, but he grabbed her hand and wrestled with her until she stopped.

"Let's mind our manners now. Be a good little girl and finish your ice cream so we can go shopping."

They both looked up to see the fat lady staring at them. "Nice dress," Billy said, pulling Holly off the bench.

"Well, what do you think?" he asked her as they stood in a toy store.

64

"Oh, Billy, it's absolutely adorable!"

It was a little brown dog operated by remote control. With the push of a button, it would bark, walk, and even sit up and beg.

"Good. This is what I'm getting. I just wanted to be sure."

"Who's it for?"

He was evasive. "Just a friend."

"How old?"

Billy didn't even know Pete's age. "I dunno. Six or seven, I guess."

Holly thought the child might be too old for the toy. But it was obvious that Billy had made up his mind, so she didn't voice her opinion. She looked at her watch. "Oh my gosh! Mickey's got one hand on the four and one hand on the six! We gotta go. Miss Connors will have a hissy-fit!"

❖ ❖ ❖

On Fridays, all the cheer squads worked out on the football field as the team practiced in the background. Miss Connors was more than a little surprised to see Holly running onto the field.

"Your leg's better!"

"I swear, Miss Connors, it's a miracle! It doesn't hurt at all."

"Oh," she said, raising her eyes thankfully to the sky, "this is wonderful!"

Holly looked over Miss Connors' shoulder. Jeff was standing on the sidelines, his helmet in his hand, looking at her. Ryan came up from behind and smacked him playfully on the back of the head. "Are you in love, or what?"

65

"She's cute, isn't she?" he asked, waving to Holly.

"Naw. She's ugly," Ryan laughed.

Jeff gave chase and tackled him. Holly watched amusedly as the two of them rolled around on the grass like a couple of playful puppies. The butterflies in her stomach were beginning again.

Coach Howard's whistle broke the spell, and Holly watched Jeff and Ryan get up quickly and run onto the field. They were doing drills, and Jeff was playing offense. Doug was playing defense and took the field opposite Jeff on the far end of the line. The coach blew the whistle to begin the drill. Holly watched, horrified, as Doug charged across the field and attacked Jeff, knocking the wind out of him before he knew what hit him.

It happened so fast, the team just stood there until Jeff caught his breath. When he tried to get up, Doug slugged him in the face.

Ryan jumped on Doug, pinning his arms behind his back as the coach ran onto the field.

Doug was yelling, "You made a fool outta me last night!"

Jeff shook off the sting, rubbing his jaw.

"What's going on?" Coach Howard demanded.

"This fruitcake's in my face!" Doug said angrily.

The coach turned to Jeff. "What's this all about, Reynolds?"

Jeff jerked free of his grasp. "Nothin'! It's about nothin'!"

Doug and Jeff glared at each other as the coach waited for an explanation. When there was none, he said, "Okay, I don't know what this is all about, but we've got a game tonight and we need both of your

66

heads in it! Whatever's eatin' you guys, leave it alone, got it?"

They continued to glare at each other angrily.

"Got it?" the coach shouted.

"Yeah," Jeff said reluctantly.

"Jetty, what about you?"

"Okay."

"All right. You guys go to the showers and cool off. And *listen*: I don't want either of you to so much as *breathe* in the other guy's direction, you hear me?"

Holly resisted the temptation to run across the field. After all, she hardly knew Jeff. It wasn't as if they were boyfriend and girlfriend or anything.

He saw her staring and waved, a little embarrassed, signaling that he was all right. She waved back and took her place in the cheer line.

Sandy talked all through the routine, making it impossible for Holly to concentrate. "I swear, someone ought to make mincemeat outta Doug Jetty's face! What a jerk! Lindsey said Jeff asked you to Ryan's party tonight. Aren't you excited? You'll probably be the only sophomore there!"

"*Miss Yates!* Stop that incessant talking!" Miss Connors demanded.

"Yes, Miss Connors." Then she added quickly, under her breath, "See, Holly? What'd I tell you? She *hates* me!"

The street in front of Ryan's house was lined on both sides with cars. Kids were standing around in the yard, and some had perched themselves like ornaments on the hoods of their cars, laughing and talking.

"Cindy will be here," Jeff warned. "Are you ready for that?"

"Yes."

"Are you sure? You'll probably be the only under-classman here."

"I'm not worried."

He turned to her. "You're terrific, you know that?"

She didn't want him to know it, but she was more than a little worried. She'd heard rumors about how vicious Cindy could be. Not only that, but Jeff and Cindy had gone together so long that they were almost a tradition at Kennedy High. Holly was smart enough to know that some of the kids would never accept anyone but Cindy as Jeff's date. She took a deep breath, confident that whatever happened, a date with Jeff Reynolds was well worth it.

The front door was open, and the party noise floated out into the front yard. "They started without us!" he said.

Holly tried to look horrified. "Imagine the nerve!"

Laughing, they went inside.

The house was stuffed to the corners with kids. Some were on the floor in front of the coffee table, munching the pretzels and potato chips put there thoughtfully by Mrs. Cummins. Others were in the kitchen or sitting on the staircase, and kids were crammed shoulder to shoulder in the narrow hallways. Cindy and Doug were on the couch, and Doug had his arm around her.

When Cindy saw Holly and Jeff come in, she snuggled closer to Doug. He tried to kiss her, but she pulled away quickly. Holly could tell by the expression on her face that Doug repulsed her. Holly couldn't imagine even sitting next to Doug Jetty, let alone *kissing* him. She shuddered involuntarily at the thought of it.

"Let's go find Ryan," Jeff said, pulling her toward the kitchen.

Cindy followed them, pretending to need another soft drink. Several of her friends were standing in the doorway, eager to see what would happen. She whispered something to them, and immediately, they all looked at Holly and laughed loudly.

Holly felt as strange as a two-legged dog. *How am I ever going to get through this?* she wondered. She wished Lindsey was there. Most of all, she wished Billy was there, so she could have a drink to calm her nerves.

Jeff held her hand tightly and gave her a wink. "Don't worry about them. It's not worth it."

Ryan was at the sink, cracking trays of ice into a bowl. When he saw Jeff, he dumped the ice, ran across the room, and jumped on Jeff's back. "You're awesome! What a game tonight! Those sportswriters at *The Daily News* will never call us underdogs again."

Jeff mussed Ryan's hair and said to Holly, "This guy's the head of my fan club."

"*Three* touchdowns! You were awesome!" Ryan repeated, jumping down.

All the kids in the kitchen had stopped what they were doing when Jeff came in. They were listening as Ryan praised his performance on the football field. And *Holly* was *his* date. In spite of Cindy, she had never felt so important.

Holly smiled victoriously as Cindy turned on her

heel and huffed back into the living room as if she could hear what Holly was thinking.

Ryan turned to Holly. "Hi! Wanna drink?"

"Oh, that'd be great!" she said thankfully.

"Coke or Pepsi?"

Her face fell . . . she was hoping for something stronger. She saw that Carrie and Wendell had beer, and some of the other kids had hard liquor. But since Jeff wasn't drinking alcohol, she was embarrassed to ask for any.

"Pepsi will be fine," she said. With any luck, maybe someone would give her some rum to put in it.

As Jeff held her hand, she listened intently while the boys rehashed every play of the game. After a while, nearly the whole team was gathered around Jeff. Most of the girls were left in the living room with Cindy.

"I can't believe that little witch," Cindy was saying. "She's not happy just having Jeff, now she's horning in on everyone else, too!"

Rachel Warner stretched to see into the kitchen. "She'd better not get any ideas about Randy, or I'll break her face!"

Cindy seized the opportunity to sprinkle gasoline on an already smoldering fire. "Listen, if she could get Jeff away from *me*, any one of you could be next. I think we better find something to stop little Miss Holly-Jolly in her tracks!"

Holly saw them staring. She wanted to go in with them—to be part of their group. She wanted to show the other girls that she wasn't as bad as Cindy said, but she knew that Cindy had turned them all against her. She heard only muffled parts of their conversation:

70

"witch . . . teach her a lesson . . . boyfriend stealer. . . ."

Holly felt nervous, and she had to go to the bathroom, but she sure didn't want to walk past them to get there. She'd had three Pepsis during the game.

When she just couldn't wait any longer, she took a deep breath, excused herself, and walked into the living room, toward their gawking faces.

Cindy stood up, blocking Holly's path to the hallway. "Hello, Jolly!" she said snidely.

Holly's heartbeat quickened as the other girls formed a hostile circle around her. Her hands began to tremble, partly from nervousness and partly from fear. She straightened her posture and looked Cindy directly in the eye. "My name is *Holly.* Excuse me. I need to use the rest room."

When Holly attempted to walk around her, Cindy moved, trapping Holly between her elite circle of friends and the coffee table. "I hope you're enjoying your date with *MY* boyfriend," Cindy said.

Holly's nervousness increased as, for a split second, she considered her alternatives: She could push Cindy out of the way; she could argue that Jeff was *not* Cindy's boyfriend; she could step over the coffee table; she could. . . . Finally, Holly said, "Listen, I don't want any hard feelings. I was under the impression that you and Jeff broke up. He's just a *date.* I'm sorry if. . . ."

Before she could finish her sentence, Cindy threw her soda in Holly's face.

The girls gasped in horror at what Cindy had done. "You *witch!*" Cindy said. "You'll pay for this!"

Holly was mortified. She fought back tears as the

71

sticky droplets trickled off her bangs, onto her nose, and rolled off her chin. She opened her mouth to speak, but no words would come out.

Immediately, the girls surrounded Cindy, chuckling at the sight of the pathetic, soda-drenched creature who had dared to invade their private world.

"I can't believe you did it!" Susan said, laughing. "Did you see the look on her face?"

"Well, she deserved it!"

Holly slipped past them into the hallway. There was a line waiting for the bathroom, and Holly was fourth.

Carrie Kelly, the school mascot, was in front of her. Holly knew her from gym class.

"I saw what she did," Carrie said, handing her a tissue. "You all right?" She puffed nervously on her cigarette.

Holly wiped her face and tried to make light of what had happened. "I feel like bacteria in an operating room. I don't think I'm welcome here. Thank God Jeff didn't see, it would have been twice as embarrassing!"

"Ya shoulda slugged her."

"I don't think so." She dabbed at her sweater. "Boy, she really hates me. They all hate me!"

"I wouldn't worry about it. None of them girls has two brain cells to rub together. They'd commit mass suicide if Cindy told 'em to."

"You think so?"

"I *know* so."

"Why do they go along with her? They can't all be as mean as she is."

Carrie took a pint of cherry brandy out of her purse

72

and took a swig. Then, she held the bottle out to Holly. "Go ahead. It'll calm yer nerves."

She watched Holly take a drink and then continued, "It's been the same since seventh grade. Cindy's always in control, ya know? No one questions what she does. Some of them girls are okay 'til they get around her. Then they act different. Cindy gets 'em to do things they never would otherwise. She brings out the worst in everybody."

"Then why is she so popular?"

"If you're not her friend, you're her enemy. After what happened to you tonight, you can figure out why no one wants to be her enemy!" She took another swig of the brandy.

"Once, in fifth grade," Carrie continued, "she jumped on Brenda Melroy and gave her a black eye for no reason. Brenda cried and cried, but everybody seemed to take Cindy's side, even though Brenda hadn't done anything to deserve a punch in the eye. I never could figure that one out. . . ."

She took another drink. "I can't get through one of these parties without a drink."

"Why do you come then?" Holly took the bottle again. "Umm . . . that's good."

"Wendell says it tastes like cough syrup," Carrie said, laughing. "I come 'cause Wendell's part of the team, and he likes to be here."

Wendell was the team's best—and biggest—tackle. He and Carrie had been going steady since the seventh grade. With the exception of Cindy's closest friends, everyone loved Wendell and Carrie. Neither of them was conscious of fashion or fad, neither used proper grammar or had any aspirations toward anything exceptional in life. They were just two kind, very likable people who were totally devoted to each other.

Holly thought about what Carrie said. Then she said, "Well, I can't blame her for being upset. I'm sure I'd feel the same way if I lost someone like Jeff."

Carrie swore, then said, "How can you defend her after what she done to you? Besides, Cindy don't care about Jeff. She just got her pride hurt because he threw her over for somebody else."

The bathroom door opened. Carrie took another swallow of brandy and moved up in line. "Here, take another swig. You'll feel better."

Holly giggled. "Actually, I'm feeling much better already. I could get used to this stuff! It makes you feel warm all over." She took another swallow—a bigger one this time.

"Go ahead, take all ya want. We got another bottle in the car."

Leaning back against the wall, Holly tipped the bottle, enjoying the sensation as the sweet, soothing liquid ran down her throat, warming her all the way to her stomach.

Carrie shifted back and forth uncomfortably. "Ya know, beer's a big waste of money. For the amount of time it's in your system, they oughta *rent* it to ya!" She banged on the door impatiently. "Hurry up in there, will ya? I gotta go!" She turned to Holly, frustrated over the long wait. "Whoever's in there must have a bladder the size of Dumbo!"

Holly laughed loudly and took another swallow of the brandy. She felt lightheaded and happy, and she

74

really liked the feeling. She laughed hysterically as Carrie danced a restless jig waiting for her turn in the bathroom.

The brandy was gone and all of a sudden, Holly was having a great time. Cindy and her friends didn't seem so intimidating anymore and Holly was determined to have fun. No one was going to spoil it for her!

She took her turn in the bathroom, not even caring about the sticky stains on her sweater. She splashed some cold water on her face, combed her fingers through her hair and started back toward the kitchen.

"What took you so long?" Jeff asked.

"There was a long wait for the bathroom."

He looked at her strangely. "You look funny. Are you okay? What happened to your sweater?"

"I spilled my drink," she lied. The brandy was really having an effect on her. She felt herself swooning.

"Are you sick? You look like you're gonna pass out!" He grabbed her around the waist just as her legs began to buckle underneath her.

She wrapped her arm around his shoulder, saving herself from a certain fall. "I'll be okay. Carrie gave me some brandy. I drank too much too fast, I think."

He looked at her closely, the disappointment evident on his face. He was considering how to handle the situation when she began to cry. "She *humiliated* me, Jeff! In front of *everyone*! Cindy threw her drink right in my face!"

Angrily, he shot a look past Holly into the living room at Cindy. She was on her way out the door, flanked on both sides by her friends. Doug Jetty stood dumbfounded, alone by the couch. He didn't have a clue as to what he'd done to upset her so much.

Jeff grabbed a paper towel from a roller on the wall and handed it to Holly. Her mascara was making black streaks on her face. She dabbed sloppily at her eyes.

"I'm sorry, Holly," he sympathized. "Don't worry about it, really."

She wiped her runny nose with the paper towel. "I was so *embarrassed*!" she sobbed.

"Let's go outside," he offered gently.

They sat together on the grass. It was getting cold, and Jeff put his arm around Holly. "You okay?"

"No, I feel awful! I feel like I might throw up!" She jumped up and ran behind a tree. After a few minutes, she came back and attempted to add some humor to the situation. "False alarm. I'm going to live."

He wasn't amused. "How much did you drink?"

"Too much, I guess."

He remembered how drunk some of her friends were at The Fantastic. "Do you drink like this . . . often?"

"Sometimes."

He sat silently, pulling blades of grass from the lawn.

"What's wrong?" she asked.

"Why do you do it?"

"Do what?"

"Why do you drink like that?"

She shrugged her shoulders. "Boredom, I guess. I don't know." She tugged nervously on her shoelace. "I guess I'm lonely."

"You, *lonely*? I don't believe that for a minute."

"Oh, I have friends, that's not what I mean. It's

just that, well . . . it seems like my whole life's changed lately. My parents are never home. It seems to me like I'm always alone. When I go to bed, no one's there. Even when I wake up, no one's there most of the time.

"Except for Saturday breakfast, I haven't had a meal with anyone at home for almost six weeks! It's *lonely* there!

"I'm pretty used to my dad being gone, but not my mom. My mom's always been home. Even though she works, she always arranged her schedule so she'd be home when I got there. I really liked that, knowing that she'd be home. She's always taken an interest in what I do. But lately, it's like neither of them even knows I exist. It's like they don't even think I *need* them anymore!" She sounded so sad that Jeff had to resist the temptation to cradle her in his arms. "I know it sounds weird, but I *miss* my parents. They seem to care more about their careers than they do about me."

"Why don't you tell them how you feel?"

"I try to, but they don't hear me."

"Is there any other reason why you decided to drink tonight?"

She smiled widely. "You're so sweet! You really want to know?"

"Yeah, I really want to know."

She liked him so much. He was so kind, so gentle, and his concern was genuine. "I've never been treated the way Cindy treated me tonight. It was horrible! No matter what a person did to me, I could *never* be that mean!"

He looked at her adoringly. He believed her. Though Holly didn't know it, Jeff had admired her for a long time. He'd taken every opportunity to find out everything he could about her. For several weeks, he'd asked others who knew her to tell him what she was like.

He'd never heard anyone say anything uncomplimentary about Holly Henderson. He'd found out that she was soft-spoken and always seemed happy. She had a natural sweetness and compassion that drew kids to her. And she accepted everyone just as they were. No one ever felt that he had to win Holly's approval. Kids knew they could be Holly's friend with no conditions attached and that put very special value on her friendship. There was nothing fake or pretentious about her. She was just . . . Holly. He felt like he was falling in love with her, and he hardly knew her.

He wanted to go on seeing her, but her drinking concerned him. . . . Most of the kids drank alcohol, and no one thought much about it. It was pretty much accepted. The few kids who didn't drink—Jeff included—were considered weird by the ones who did. Jeff was very aware that some of the football players called him names behind his back. "Goody-goody," "Jesus freak," and "Mr. Perfect" were a few he'd heard. Some accused him of being self-righteous and thinking he was better than everyone else because he didn't participate in their drinking games and saw nothing humorous about a hangover.

He could have let the name calling anger him, but he thought that was a waste of emotion. He questioned whether those who called people names were even worth his effort. After all, they'd formed opinions of him without any interest in his reasons. They assumed that he didn't drink because, to quote Doug Jetty, he was a "Bible-thumpin' Jesus freak." But that wasn't exactly true.

Jeff's choice had nothing to do with his thinking he was better than they were. And the fact that he was a Christian was only one reason he chose not to drink. Anyone who cared enough to ask would have known that he had always hated the taste of alcohol, and he hated even more what it did to people.

Also, Jeff was an athlete seeking a college scholarship. He was dependent on his physical ability to get him through school, because his parents sure couldn't afford to send him. He felt that abusing his body with drugs or alcohol could cost him a college education.

To Jeff, his decision not to drink seemed logical and intelligent. Why was it such a big deal to some people? He didn't understand why so many kids would drink just because they thought it was expected of them. It just didn't make sense to him at all. He'd learned in his psychology course that people who drank a lot did it because they had some deeper problem they couldn't handle. Doug Jetty got drunk every weekend. Jeff thought it was because he had a need to prove his masculinity. Somehow, guys like Doug thought manhood was measured by how crass and obnoxious one could be.

Ryan, Jeff's best friend, used to get drunk whenever his parents had one of their terrible fights. Jeff spent a lot of time talking with him, and gradually Ryan stopped getting drunk. Instead, Ryan came to rely on Jeff, who was always willing to listen when his friend was troubled.

Jeff noticed, too, that a lot of girls who didn't think

79

very much of themselves drank a lot. These were the girls who by outward appearances were popular, but inside, he thought they were consumed with worry about what others were thinking and saying about them. Most of them tended to be very judgmental of others, so they automatically thought that others were the same way with them.

But Holly wasn't like anyone else. Jeff couldn't figure her out. He wanted to understand why she had the need to drink, so he listened intently while she continued.

"I wanted to get even with Cindy for throwing that drink in my face, but I was afraid. When Carrie offered me the brandy, I took it because I thought if I drank enough, I'd have the nerve to stand up to her. I didn't mean to get drunk."

"You must have been really embarrassed, but . . ." he hesitated, measuring his words carefully. He didn't want to offend her. "It's just that I . . . well, I don't think drinking is a good way to deal with problems. There are other ways to handle things, that's all."

"Like how? Murder's against the law. . . ."

"Like Jesus," he said boldly.

She thought he was joking. "Are you serious?"

There was no mistaking the look of commitment in his eyes. "Yes, I'm very serious. What do you think about spiritual things?"

"I don't know what to say," she said honestly. "I guess I don't think much of anything about spiritual things . . . or Jesus. My family hasn't gone to church in a long time." She tugged thoughtfully at the grass. No one had ever asked her such a question before—not even Lindsey. "What do you think about spiritual things?"

He reared back and playfully tossed a handful of grass in her face. "Sometime I'll tell you what I believe. But not right now." He took her by the hand and helped her to her feet. He stood facing her and gently brushed some tiny blades of grass off her shoulder. "Holly, I wish you wouldn't drink. It won't solve any of your problems."

Before she knew it, he leaned over and kissed her sweetly on the lips.

Instinctively, she closed her eyes. It was the most beautiful kiss she'd ever experienced. She kept her eyes closed even after the kiss was over. She was afraid that if she opened them, the spell would be broken. She wanted to remember every single second with him. When she finally opened her eyes, he was smiling at her.

CHAPTER SIX

Peter Hollis sat in his wheelchair, smiling at the yapping little mechanical dog.

"It was so sweet of you, Billy," Mrs. Hollis said. "It's perfect. What ever made you think of it?"

"Well, I knew he could use his fingers a little bit, so I thought the remote would be a good idea. You know, it kinda gives him the feeling he's doing something for himself."

"It's perfect!" She put a gentle hand on Billy's shoulder. "You're such a sweet kid. . . . You'll never know how much Pete looks forward to your visits." The boy stared blankly into space. "He looks like he doesn't know what's going on, but he does."

"Sure he does, don't you Pete? You know everything that's goin' on, don't ya?" Billy was on his knees next to the wheelchair. There was a glimmer of recognition in the little boy's eyes.

"He loves you, Billy. I can see it in his eyes."

"I love you too, Pete. And so does ol' Bowser here. Don't ya, Bowser?" He took the remote and pushed the button. The dog sat up and barked. "See, I told you!" He put the little dog in the boy's lap. "There, you hold him while I read a story. And be careful—he's not housebroken yet!"

Mrs. Hollis went to get ready for the movies. Billy's visits were as much a treat for her as they were for Pete because they allowed her a chance to get out of the house. She thanked God for Billy. As Mrs. Hollis went to her room, she remembered that first time Billy came into their lives.

Back when Billy took a paper route at the age of thirteen, the Hollis' house was on his route. One day when Billy delivered the paper, Pete was sitting outside in his wheelchair. Billy felt sad for the little boy who was all crippled and hunched over, so he got off his bike and went over to talk to him. When he didn't respond, Billy said, "What's the matter, don't you like me? I like you. Why don't you talk to me?"

The boy's eyes were dark and expressive. Billy could tell that he wanted to talk. He just couldn't.

About a week after that first meeting, Billy saw Pete outside again. He went up to the front door and asked Mrs. Hollis if it would be all right for him to come back after school and visit her little boy. That was almost three years ago, and Billy had come at least twice a month ever since.

Sarah Hollis came out, ready to go.

She was a tiny-framed woman, no more than five feet tall. Her arms were thin but well-defined from lifting Pete in and out of the wheelchair. Though Billy

84

guessed she was in her late twenties, she looked frail and tired.

He studied her carefully as she searched her purse for lipstick. She was plain—more cute than pretty. Billy wondered if her husband had left her for someone more glamorous, or if he simply left because he couldn't deal with the condition of his only son. Whatever the reason, Billy thought it was a lousy thing to do.

He stood up. "You look nice."

She blushed, smoothing her skirt. She never thought about her looks anymore. There was really no reason to.

"Why, thank you. You're sure you'll be all right now?"

"Sure. Did you feed him?"

"All done. All you have to do is change him and put him to bed."

"Have a good time, and don't hurry back. We'll get along, won't we Pete?"

The little boy blinked, and Billy took that to mean "Yes."

Holly ran down the stairs to the breakfast table and threw her arms around her father, almost knocking his coffee cup out of his hand. "Whoa, little filly! Ya dern near spilled my java!" He set the cup down as he stood and gave her a big hug and kiss.

She hugged him tightly, smothering his handsome face with kisses. "I missed you! The show was great this week! Wait 'til I tell you about Jeff. I had a date with him last night, Daddy. He actually asked me out! He's the most popular boy in school, and I had a date with him! Can you believe it?"

Her mother was frying bacon. "Hey, back up a minute," she said. "What's this about having a *date* last night?"

Holly stuttered, realizing too late that she'd exposed herself. "I . . . I. . . ."

"You *what*?" Holly's mom demanded, taking the frying pan off the stove.

Holly looked to her father for help, but he offered none.

"Well, I sort of broke my restriction. You gave me permission to go to the game, so I just sort of extended your permission to include the party after the game. I know I'm supposed to be grounded, but Jeff asked me out, and I just couldn't say no!"

"I gave you permission to go to the game only because you're part of the cheer team!" Holly's mom slammed the frying pan back on the stove. "I get so frustrated with you, Holly! You *know* you were supposed to come right home afterward. . . . T. J., you handle this one!" she said, exasperated. "She's supposed to be grounded because she's been sneaking out on school nights."

He faked a German accent, "Zis iz so, fraulein?"

She giggled. "Ja, mein herr. Zis iz so."

"Well, I say, at least she's honest, so let her off the hook."

Holly's mom only acted angry. Secretly, she thought fathers had a right to spoil their daughters. "I should have known better than to leave it up to you!"

He winked at Holly.

Things were the same every single Saturday: They digested their breakfast with rapid conversation, each telling of their experiences during the past week.

Dr. Carol had them mesmerized, telling about a case involving a fourteen-year-old girl who had multiple personalities. "Dr. Weinmacher has uncovered three different personalities so far, but he thinks there are more still hidden inside. I'm counseling her parents about how to deal with it."

Holly's dad told her all the gossip from the set, some of which she already knew from reading *People* magazine. Trish's character was killed off, he said, because the actress who played the part was having an affair with the producer's husband.

He chuckled, telling them he found out that "Johnny what's-his-name" was a Buddhist who believes he's going to be reincarnated as bacteria in a glass of low-fat milk.

Holly laughed. She felt complete contentment on Saturday mornings at the breakfast table with her mom and dad.

"So," her dad encouraged, "tell us all about this ugly guy you broke all the rules to go out with."

Holly didn't even try to keep the excitement out of her voice. "Jeff's captain of the football team, student body president, and he gets straight As! He's the most handsome boy in school, and he's *so* nice I just can't believe it!"

"So," her dad kidded, "do you like him or not?"

She slugged him playfully. "Oh, Daddy!"

"It's important that he gets good grades," her mother said sensibly. "He'll probably be successful in life."

That was the furthest thing from Holly's mind, but she had to agree with her mother.

"He's real nice, Mom. Everyone likes him. He was going with a girl for a long time. . . ."

Holly's mom held up her hand, signaling Holly to stop talking. "Excuse me for just a minute, honey. . . .

"T. J., did you remember to call the dealership about getting the Mercedes serviced? They're so slow. If we don't get a time reserved soon, we may have to wait another two weeks."

He rolled his eyes back, unable to believe that he'd forgotten *again* to do what his wife requested several weeks ago. "I'll do it this afternoon."

"You can't do it this afternoon, T. J. The service department is closed on Saturdays! Honestly, I ask you to do one thing—one simple thing for me—and you forget! You know I hate to take care of the cars. We agreed that the cars are your responsibility and the gardener is mine. . . ."

"I know, I'm sorry. It's just that when I get back to Hollywood, my mind's on the show."

"Well, I know, but you've got responsibilites here, too."

The phone rang, and Holly's mom got up to answer it. She carried on an in-depth conversation, apparently with her answering service. When she sat back down, she asked Holly to continue sharing with them about Jeff.

Somewhat less enthusiastically, Holly went on: "Jeff was going with Cindy Aldrich for a long time. . . ."

"She's the head cheerleader, isn't she?"

"Uh-huh."

"I saw her at a football game. She's cute."

"She looks cute. She doesn't act so cute. She hates

88

me because she thinks I stole Jeff away from her, but he was going to break up with her anyway. Now she's trying to make my life miserable. Last night she tripped me in front of everyone!"

"Oh no!" her mother said, horrified. "That must have been embarrassing."

"I almost died! I. . . ."

The phone rang again, and Holly's mom rushed to answer it. After a brief conversation, she hung up. "I gotta go. I've got a potential suicide. Mr. Bradley's on the roof threatening to jump." She ran upstairs, dressed hurriedly, and was back in the kitchen, kissing them goodbye.

"I'll be back as soon as I can. . . ."

"Mom, I thought you didn't work on Saturdays!"

Carol Henderson was aghast. "Holly, this is a *suicide*, for heaven's sake!"

"You know Mr. Bradley'll never jump. He only threatens to do it to upset his wife."

"We don't play games with potential suicides, Holly. We take them very seriously."

"Why? Mrs. Bradley doesn't!" she said sharply.

Now Holly's mom was really aggravated. "I don't know what's gotten into you, Holly. But I'm certainly not going to stand here and argue while I have a patient perched on the twelfth story of an apartment building! I'll see you later." And she was out the door.

Holly sank into the chair while her dad began clearing the dishes. "Wanna wash or dry?" he asked.

"Neither!" she snapped.

He sat down beside her. "What's wrong?"

"What's wrong? I'll tell you what's wrong. I'm sick

89

of all Mom's patients monopolizing her time! I'm sick of hearing about Johnny what's-his-name! I'm sick of Mom working nights and you being gone all week long! I'm sick of being home alone every night! Saturday's supposed to be *my time*! You guys don't even care about me! You don't care about Jeff or the cheer competition or the B+ I got on my English test! All you care about are your precious careers!"

She ran up the stairs and into her room, slamming the door behind her.

Her dad was standing next to her before she even had a chance to sit down. "Holly, what's this all about?" he demanded.

"Daddy, haven't you been listening? Didn't you hear anything I said? You're never here. Mom's never here. I'm all *alone!* Even when you're here, you don't have time for me!" She fell onto her bed, sobbing into her pillow. "It's like you don't even care about me!"

"That's the most ridiculous thing I've ever heard. I know it's hard when I'm gone so much, but I call home at least twice a week. Holly, your mom and I both have very demanding careers. We have a lot of responsibilities. . . ."

"What about me? Aren't I a responsibility, too?"

"Well, of course you are. . . ."

"Then why don't you care about me? Why is it that every time you call me, it's to tell me *your* problems . . . *your* concerns? You never ask how I'm doing. All you do is whine about your precious job. I don't know why you even bother to come home at all!"

Holly's dad was half offended and half baffled. He didn't know what to say to her, so he didn't say anything. He just left her alone in her room, shutting the door quietly behind him.

❖ ❖ ❖

Rachel jogged up to the gym and tossed her pom-poms at Cindy's feet. "I'm exhausted! I don't *ever* remember working this hard for the cheer competition. I think Miss Connors and Mrs. Dorn have a bet going. Miss Connors really thinks the sophomore squad will score higher than we will in the finals. Hey, what're you doing here? I thought you were going shopping for your homecoming dress."

Cheer practice had been long and exhausting, but Cindy was full of energy and couldn't keep the excitement from her voice. "Jeff asked me to meet him; he said he has something to talk to me about."

"Oh my gosh, do you think he's going to ask you to go with him again?"

"I *know* he is! He never really broke up with me in the first place. He just kind of hinted that he wanted to date some other girls. I always knew he'd come back. . . .

"You know that little snot he brought to Ryan's party? She got *drunk*! You know how Jeff hates that. . . . I knew he'd regret going out with that little . . . snot! I can't wait to see the look on that brat's face when she sees me with Jeff on Monday. Oh, here he comes. . . . I'll call you later." She threw Rachel her pom-poms.

"Hi," Jeff said.

"Hello," Cindy answered coolly. One thing was for sure: she wasn't going to make it easy for him.

"Thanks for coming. I wanted to talk to you about something. . . ."

"I was waiting for this, Jeff," she interrupted. "It's just like you to come running back to me. . . ."

"Cindy! I just want my class ring back."

Her mouth dropped open. "I don't believe you!" she screamed. "You want your *ring back*?" She dug through her purse and yanked a long chain out. The ring dangled loosely from it as she waved it in front of his nose. "You've got to be kidding! You gave *me* this ring, Jeff, and you're not going to give it to anyone else!"

"I don't intend to give it to anyone else," he said calmly. "It's my class ring, and I'd like to have it back. I can't afford to buy another one, and I'm sure you don't want to keep it since we're not even dating anymore."

Her chest was heaving. She was so frustrated, she could hardly think straight. She was an A-student; she was head cheerleader and—she *knew*—a shoo-in for homecoming queen. She was *certainly* the prettiest girl at Kennedy High—everyone said so! How could he even think of breaking up with her? It just didn't make sense. What would people think? What would everyone *say*?

She could scarcely bear to think of herself without Jeff. He was the most popular guy in school. There was no one as good as Jeff. Who would she go with?

And homecoming was only a couple of weeks away . . . all the decent guys were taken! She couldn't stand the thought of anyone else being seen with Jeff.

She tried to calm herself down. "I'm warning you, Jeff, I'm not going to take much more of this."

They'd been through this several times before. If he left it up to Cindy, they'd probably be having this same conversation in some nursing home when they reached the ripe old age of eighty.

"Cindy, I don't want to hurt your feelings, but I really want my ring back. We've gone together a long time, and I think it would be good for you to date other people."

"But I don't *want* anyone else. I want you! You're the captain of the football team! You're the president of the student body!"

When she looked in his eyes, she knew he wouldn't change his mind. This time it was really over. "I'll tell you what," she said sweetly. "Since you already promised to take me to homecoming, I'll return your ring after the dance." She was certain that once she was crowned queen, he'd change his mind.

"I think I'd really rather. . . ."

"You're taking Brenda out tonight, aren't you?" she asked, changing the subject.

"Yes."

"She'll bore you to death. She talks too much," Cindy criticized.

"Cindy, I'd like to get my ring back."

"It just wouldn't be fair for you to back out now," she whined. "Besides, everyone will expect the queen to be with the captain of the football team."

Jeff was no good at things like this. He really didn't want to hurt her feelings. He just wanted his ring back. *Why is she always so difficult?* he wondered.

He knew she'd make a scene if he refused her. And knowing Cindy, he wouldn't have been surprised if she took his class ring and chucked it into the dumpster next to the gym . . . he'd *never* find it!

The dance was only two weeks away. And Holly

probably already had a date anyway. "Okay. You got a date."

She flung the ring back into her purse. "Wear a blue cummerbund. I don't want you clashing with my dress."

❖ ❖ ❖

Saturday afternoons were dead at the Burger Palace, but that's why Lindsey and Holly liked it. It was as if it were their own private place. Holly had already told her about Cindy throwing the soda in her face. Lindsey squirmed as if she were sitting on a swarm of red ants. "Then what happened?"

Holly was just ready to tell Lindsey about her conversation with Jeff when she saw Billy out of the corner of her eye. He came over and slid into the booth next to Lindsey. "So, will you go out with me tonight or not?"

Lindsey was losing patience. "If I go out with you tonight, will you promise *never* to ask me again, as long as you live?"

"Promise."

"Okay. Where do you want to go?"

"The zoo," he said, looking at Holly. "I used to take my old girlfriend there all the time."

Holly shook her head slowly from side to side. "Billy, you're pathetic!" She turned to Lindsey: "I went to the zoo with him once, when I was in third grade."

"We had a great time!" he said.

"Yeah," Holly said dryly, "it was great. A goat ate a hole in his Gumby shirt."

"Honestly, Billy," Lindsey said, "why don't you just apologize to Christine and be done with it?"

94

"Her mom's totally mad. I don't think she'll ever let me near their house again."

"Well, who could blame her? My mom would be mad too if you threw up all over her new carpet!"

"So I was sick . . . sue me!"

"You weren't sick. You were *drunk*. There's a big difference."

"Well, I can't help it. I have more fun when I drink."

"How do you tell the difference? You're never sober anymore!"

"I'm sober now."

"Well, if you plan on taking *me* out tonight, you'd better stay that way, because I don't get in a car with anyone who's been drinking. I mean it."

"You're serious, aren't you?"

"Believe it!"

"Well, okay. But I'll probably be dull as an old kitchen knife."

"Can you pick me up at seven?"

Billy had promised Mrs. Hollis he'd come by and stay with Pete while she went to get her groceries. "How about eight? I've gotta do something first."

"What?"

"I gotta go see a friend. I'll be there by eight. Wear something awesome."

He got up to leave, and Lindsey called after him: "Since we're going to the zoo, I'll wear my tiger-print dress and a pair of alligator shoes. I'll look gr-r-eat, Billy. I'm not lion!"

Holly rolled her eyes and sank down in the booth. "That's bad, Lins!"

95

"Who do you suppose he's going to see?" Lindsey wondered.

"I think he's got a new girlfriend. There's someone he sees a lot, and he won't tell me who it is."

"But if he's got a girlfriend, why's he taking me out instead of her?"

"I dunno." Then Holly pointed out the window. *"Oh no!"*

"What's the matter?"

"It's the entire senior cheer squad. They're coming in here."

Holly and Lindsey watched them through the window. They were all dressed in jeans and carried pom-poms.

"I can't believe it!" Holly said. "I managed to ditch Cindy all morning at practice, and now she's got to come *here*."

The girls were laughing and talking loudly as they entered the resturant, but Holly pretended not to notice them.

Cindy wasn't about to let her get by with that—not when the odds were six to two in her favor. They surrounded the table immediately. "Well, look who's here, girls! It's little Miss Holly-Jolly and her faithful side-kick, dog face!"

With her mouth full of soda, Lindsey faked a robust laugh and spit Coke all over Cindy's cheerleading sweater. "Oh my gosh, Cindy, I'm *so sorry*! It's just that . . . well, you're so funny, I couldn't help it." She and Holly stood up, both of them handing Cindy napkins as Lindsey said, "We'd love to stay and chat, but Holly doesn't want to keep *Jeff* waiting. . . ."

They strolled past the girls with the cool and easy stride of two sophisticated beauty queens. When they were safely outside, they ran as fast as they could down Meeker Street, laughing all the way.

Holly wished Lindsey wouldn't have agreed to go to the zoo with Billy, leaving her all alone on a Saturday night.

She gave a soft whistle as her parents came down the stairs dressed to kill. "You guys look great!"

She wished she was going to dinner with them, but she wasn't invited. She was never invited on Saturday nights. For as long as Holly could remember, Saturday night was "date night" for her mom and dad. Holly used to think the idea was sort of romantic, but as her parents grew more involved in their careers and spent less and less time with her, she began to resent their dates and to view them as just one more way they could avoid spending time with her.

"Why don't you come along?" her father invited.

She knew he only asked her as an afterthought, because he felt guilty about the things she said that morning. "No thanks. I'm not ready. Besides, you guys need time alone. Have a good time."

"You sure you don't want to come along?" her mother asked.

"Yeah. Maybe next time." Holly's voice sounded sad.

"Is something wrong, honey?"

Holly wanted to tell them to wait . . . that she'd get dressed and go along so they could all talk. She wanted to tell them how frightened she was just thinking of what Cindy might do next to embarrass her. And she wanted to tell them she wished they could spend time together, the three of them, like they used to. But instead, she just smiled and said, "I'm fine. See you later."

She'd been so busy all, day she'd hardly had time to think about the events the night before at Ryan's party. Now, the memory was like an unwanted guest invading her privacy.

Holly'd never experienced that kind of rejection before. It was a sad, lonesome feeling, being ganged up on like that. She felt a new kind of sympathy for kids like Ronald T. North and Henrietta Wallingsford. They were some of the less fortunate: not attractive, not socially adept or aware, and certainly not accepted.

Henrietta was overweight, sloppy, and terribly shy. Ronald was skinny, had a horrible case of acne, and a plastic pen holder to keep ink stains from spoiling the nice white shirts he kept buttoned to the collar. They were, for all intents and purposes at Kennedy High, outcasts. Though Holly never made fun of them herself, they and others like them were ridiculed thoughtlessly and constantly. For the first time in her life, Holly knew just a little bit of what that felt like.

She walked around the big, empty house, picking up things and putting them back. She decided to dust the living room and continued on into the den and dining room. *Oh, well,* she thought, *I might as well vacuum.*

After a while, she turned on the television, restlessly flicking the channels by remote control. Finally, she flicked it off and picked up the latest copy of *Vogue.*

Whenever Holly asked her mother to buy her a magazine, her mother always picked *Vogue,* even though Holly had told her she didn't like it. She licked her thumb and turned a few of the pages listlessly before she threw the magazine on the floor. She hated *Vogue* because kids never dressed like that. Why couldn't her mother buy *Seventeen* instead?

She put her head back on a sofa pillow and closed her eyes, remembering. . . . Even as a tiny child, Holly's mother had always treated her as an adult. Holly reasoned that it had something to do with her mother's interest in psychology.

Whenever Holly asked her mother for permission to do something, Carol Henderson would never just say "yes" or "no." She always had to explain the positive and negative aspects, and then she encouraged her tiny daughter to decide her fate for herself.

Once when Holly was about three years old, her mother was baking cookies around the holidays. Holly kept begging her for more and more cookies. Her mother never said "no," but she did tell Holly, "If you don't stop eating, you'll get sick." Holly kept right on eating until she got so sick, she was doubled over the toilet, throwing up.

Remembering, Holly shuddered at the mere thought of a frosted sugar cookie.

She got up and, out of sheer boredom, went to the bar and searched through the bottles. She was surprised to find a bottle of cherry brandy. She filled a snifter and picked up the magazine again. When she'd finished looking through it, she'd finished the brandy.

99

She poured another one and decided to give Carrie a call.

Carrie and Wendell were at the movies, Carrie's mother said.

Fine. I'll drink by myself, Holly thought. She turned on the TV, plopped down on the couch, and began flicking the channels around with the remote control. She went around the channels a few times, found nothing of interest, so clicked the set off. She lay down on the couch, closed her eyes and thought about changing clothes and going over to The Fantastic to meet the girls. Yeah, maybe she'd do that . . . that sounded like fun. She emptied the snifter and poured herself a third one. She decided to go over the cheer routines once more, and then she'd get dressed and go dancing!

Holly was head cheerleader for the sophomore squad. The sophomores had never finished higher in the cheer finals than the seniors. But Miss Connors told Holly that this year the sophomore cheer squad was the best Kennedy High had ever had. Miss Connors was certain that the sophomores would win the state title. Holly couldn't wait to see the look on Cindy's face when that happened!

Holly got her pom-poms and danced around the living room, kicking her legs so high she feared for the safety of the chandelier. She jumped and kicked and twirled and pranced, until she thought she'd drop dead from exhaustion. Then, she went to the refrigerator and got herself an ice-cold beer.

She called Sandy's house, but she was at Kevin's. She dialed Melissa's number and then remembered

100

that she and Christine had gone to The Fantastic. "Oh, yeah, I could go dancing too!" Holly laughed at her lapse of memory.

She looked in the refrigerator but there was nothing to eat that pleased her. She was feeling a little lightheaded, so she had a bowl of pretzels. The pretzels made her thirsty, so she had another bottle of beer. And, as she drank, she fell asleep on the couch.

❖ ❖ ❖

Jeff tried to act interested in Brenda's conversation, but the fact was, he couldn't get Holly Henderson off his mind. He kept thinking of the conversation he'd had with her at Ryan's party. He was feeling sorry for her, wondering how she was.

Finally, Brenda stopped talking and asked Susan if she needed to go to the ladies' room.

After the girls left, Ryan said, "What's with you tonight? It's like you're on another planet."

"I wish I was with Holly," he said honestly.

"Well, ask her out again, stupid!"

❖ ❖ ❖

Holly was awakened by the ringing of the phone. She felt dazed and groggy.

"Hello?"

"Holly? It's Jeff. . . ." He was relieved that she had answered the phone. That meant she wasn't out with someone else.

She sat bolt upright and smoothed her hair, as if he could see her right through the receiver.

"Oh . . . hi, Jeff!"

101

"You sound funny. Are you okay?"

"I was asleep. What time is it?"

"Nine-thirty."

"Nine-thirty?" It felt like midnight at least. Her head hurt.

"Yeah, *nine-thirty*! What're you doing sleeping at nine-thirty on a Saturday night?" he teased.

"My parents went out. There's nothing to do. . . . I fell asleep on the couch. What're you doing?"

"Nothing really. How's everything?"

She knew he was referring to her confrontation with Cindy the night before. "I'm okay. I managed to avoid her at cheer practice." She didn't think it was necessary to mention what happened at the Burger Palace. "Would you like to come over and watch some TV or something? My folks went out to dinner, and I'm just sitting here. . . ."

The question surprised him, and he wasn't prepared with an answer. It would be mean to tell her he was on a date with someone else.

Embarrassed by the silence, Holly finally said, "Hey, listen, if you can't make it. . . ."

"I can't tonight," he confessed, "but another time for sure. What's a pretty girl like you doin' sitting home on Saturday night, anyway?"

"Maybe I'm not so pretty after all," she suggested.

"Not true! Wanna go out with me again?"

"Sure!"

"Great. Well, I guess I'll see you at school on Monday."

"Bye." She hung up the phone and sank back onto the couch. He wanted to be with *her*. And she wanted to

102

be with him. She'd have given *anything* to be with him right then.

Her excitement turned to concern as she guessed that he was probably on a date with someone else. She wondered if it was Cindy.

Suddenly, she lost her desire to go dancing. The thought of Jeff with someone else was just too depressing. She couldn't remember ever having feelings like this for anyone. He was the first thing she thought of when she woke up, and Lindsey had accused her of talking of nothing but Jeff all day long.

I'm being stupid, she thought to herself. *I've only had one date with him. It's not like we're going together or anything. I'm just one of the girls he dates. I'm making a fool of myself.*

She whimpered out loud and, turning, flung herself face down on the couch. She wondered who he was with. What if it was Cindy? She wished her parents would come home so she'd have someone to talk to. She felt so depressed . . . she felt like she didn't have anyone. . . .

Grandma Rachel's clock was ticking its same, lonesome sound. If it hadn't been for that constant tick-tock, Holly swore she would have heard her heart breaking.

CHAPTER SEVEN

Lindsey ran down the hall and grabbed Holly's arm, spinning her around. "You won! You *won!*"

Holly's eyes opened wide and her mouth fell open. "No way!"

"I just saw it. The names are posted in the window at the attendance office. It's right there in black and white: Sophomore Princess—Holly Henderson!"

"Oh my gosh, I just don't believe it!"

Melissa, Sandy, and Christine were all gathered around her now, screaming happily and jumping up and down. "Aren't you excited?" Christine asked. "What are you going to wear? Did you pick out a dress yet?"

"No, I was afraid I'd jinx myself."

"Are you going to ask Jeff to take you?" Sandy asked.

"Cindy already asked him."

Sandy said, "Well, he might be taking her to the dance, but they won't be doing the 'Queen's Waltz'!"

Holly looked puzzled. "What's that supposed to mean?"

"Cindy didn't win!" Sandy said gleefully.

"No way! She always wins everything!"

"Well, she didn't win homecoming queen. Brenda won! And you know what else? You're gonna *love* this! . . . She didn't even win senior princess. Rachel won!"

"*What*? I don't believe it! She'll die! Oh, this is terrible. I mean, it's too bad for Cindy, but it's great for Brenda and Rachel," Holly said sincerely.

"Too bad? Are you crazy? After all she's done to you. . . . This is the best thing that ever happened!" Lindsey said. "There's a meeting in fifteen minutes in the gym—for the queen and her court, one of which is you. They're going to be taking pictures for the paper."

Holly was so excited, she could hardly stand it. She hurried into the rest room to fix her hair and makeup for the pictures. Cindy was in there, and she was crying.

Holly's first inclination was to leave, but she couldn't. She walked closer and put her hand on Cindy's arm. "Are you all right?"

Cindy pulled away. "Leave me alone!"

"Cindy, I'm sorry you didn't win, but it's not the end of the world."

"It *is* the end of the world! My parents expected me to win. I *always* win, and I would have won this time if it hadn't been for you!"

"Me? What did I have to do with it?"

"You told everyone not to vote for me. You turned them all against me!"

"That's not true. I wouldn't do that."

"It *is* true, you liar!" She was sobbing hysterically.

106

Instead of anger, Holly felt pity. How could it be so important? She got a paper towel wet and handed it to Cindy. "Here, your mascara's running."

Cindy jerked the wet towel from her hand.

Holly laid her purse and books on the sink. "I didn't realize winning was so important to you."

"Winning's the *only* thing that's important!"

"There'll be other contests. . . ."

"Not like this one! This is homecoming, you idiot! I'm a senior. This is my *last* homecoming—my last chance to be queen! Don't you understand *anything*?"

"I'm sorry you lost," Holly repeated softly.

"You miserable liar! Do you expect me to believe that? You're the reason I lost. It's all your fault! You stuffed the ballot box, and I know it! I've never hated anyone as much as I hate you! And once Jeff finds out what you did, he'll hate you too and so will everyone else in school!"

Finally, Holly'd had enough. "Listen to me, Cindy. You can think anything you want, but I had nothing to do with your losing the contest. Maybe you lost because people are sick of you running everything. Or maybe you lost because you tripped one person too many or stabbed the wrong person in the back! I don't know why you lost, but it *wasn't* because of me!"

"Well, I sure don't know why *you* won! The sophomore class must be really hard up to vote for someone like you!"

"I won that contest fair and square, and you lost the same way! And I'm sure not going to let anything you say spoil it for me!"

But the fact was that everything was already

spoiled as far as Holly was concerned.

Brenda was the first person to greet Holly as she came into the gym. She threw her arms around her and hugged her warmly. "Congratulations, Holly. I'm really happy for you!"

Holly knew she meant it. "Thanks, Brenda, I'm happy for you, too."

"You sure don't sound happy!"

"I just saw Cindy. She's pretty upset about losing."

"Well, she's used to winning."

"Hey, Brenda, do you . . ." she stopped mid-sentence.

"What?"

"Oh, never mind. I was just wondering if. . . ."

"*What?*"

Holly began to cry.

"What's wrong with you, Holly?" Brenda took her arm, and together they went behind the stage. "Holly, what is it?"

"Oh, Brenda, I feel so bad!" she sobbed. "Cindy thinks I turned everyone against her. She even accused me of stuffing the ballot box!"

"That's the most ridiculous thing I've ever heard. Everyone knows you wouldn't do that."

"By the time she's through she'll probably have the whole school believing I did!"

"Honestly, Holly, you're making too much of this. Can't you see what she's doing? She's jealous! No one's going to believe you'd do anything like that—especially when the accusations come from a sore loser."

"You really think so?"

"I know so! Now wipe your face. They're here to take our picture."

108

❖ ❖ ❖

Holly ran all the way home. She couldn't wait to tell her mother that she'd been elected homecoming princess and her picture was going to be in the newspaper. She threw open the front door and shouted inside, forgetting that her mother was at the radio station. *"Mom! Mom . . . ?* Oh, shoot!" She ran to the phone and waited impatiently for her mother to answer.

"Mom, guess what? I won sophomore princess!"

"That's wonderful, Holly."

She'd expected more of a reaction. Obviously, her mother didn't realize just how big a deal this was. "Can we get my dress tomorrow?"

"Honey, you know I'm working. . . ."

Holly's face fell. "Can't you take some time off?"

"I can't do that. You know how backed up I am right now because of this radio program."

"But, Mom, this is important!"

"So is my job."

"Yeah, it's more important to you than I am, that's for sure!"

"Holly!"

"You know it's true! You'd rather be on the radio, giving advice to people you don't even know. What about *me*? What about doing something for me?"

Holly's mother was speechless. Holly seldom got upset about anything. She was so even-tempered and happy, she was almost abnormal in her mother's eyes. Finally she said, "Holly, what's wrong with you? You've been so moody lately. . . . Why did you snap at me like that?"

Holly rolled her eyes. She wanted to shout into

109

the receiver: "Because you ignore me! Because you're too busy to care about me!" But instead, she said, "I'm just disappointed. I thought you'd want to take me to get my dress. . . ."

"Holly, it's not fair to say that I don't want to take you. I *can't* take you! Ask Lindsey . . . I'm sure she'd love to go with you."

"Can you take me Saturday?"

"Honey, I'm sorry, the station booked me for a public appearance. It's not 'til noon though. I could take you before I go. I'd have to be home by 11:30 so I could change and get over to the hotel. . . ."

"The stores don't even open 'til ten. I can't pick out a dress for the most important day of my life in an hour and a half!"

Holly's mother's temper was rising. She'd like to take her daughter shopping, but there was no way she could get out of her speaking engagement. "What do you expect me to do?"

"Just tell them you can't do it!"

"I can't do that, Holly. They're expecting me. The publicity's been done. Besides, they couldn't possibly find another speaker at this late date!"

"You could get out of it if you wanted!"

"No, I can't! I can't get out of it, and you're being very unreasonable about the whole thing! Why did you wait until the last minute to find a dress, anyway?"

Holly's voice was quiet and sad. "Because I didn't think I'd win. . . . It's okay, Mom. You don't have to take me if you don't want to. I'll call Lindsey."

"Holly, I told you. It's not that I don't want to take you. . . ."

"I said it's okay! Just forget it, all right?" She slammed the phone on the cradle.

Holly's mom dialed her back immediately, but Holly refused to answer the phone. She felt sorry for herself and angry with her mother. This was the most important thing that had ever happened to her, and her mother was too busy. She wished her dad were home. Maybe at least he'd show a little interest.

She heard a soft knock. When she opened the front door, Billy presented her with a pink rose. It was surrounded by a delicate spray of baby's-breath and tied with a pink satin ribbon.

She looked endearingly at him. "Oh, Billy, you're so sweet! What's this for?"

"It's the least I can do for a *princess.*"

She took him by the arm as he walked inside. "I'm so glad to see you. You always show up at just the right time."

"I'm glad you won."

"Thank you. You're so sweet!" she repeated.

"I thought we ought to celebrate. Are your folks home?"

"They're *never* home!"

He pulled a bottle of rum from his jacket pocket. "Got any sweet stuff to go with this?"

She smiled widely. "Oh, this is great! I'll be right back. I'm gonna call Lindsey."

She dialed the phone quickly. "Lins, can you come over? Billy's got some rum, and we're gonna celebrate my princess-hood!"

Lindsey looked at the clock on the kitchen wall. It was 3:35. This was just too much, even for Holly.

111

If she didn't watch it, she'd be just like Billy. "You're drinking *now*?"

"Yeah." Holly looked at the grandfather clock and giggled. "It's cocktail time someplace." She winked at Billy.

Lindsey couldn't keep the worry out of her voice: "Holly, are you sure you want to drink now?"

"Yes! Are you coming over or not?"

"*Not*. I'm working on my science project. It's due on Monday. What's yours on?"

"Mine's on 'hold.' I haven't even started it yet."

"Holly, it's due *next Monday*! It's one-third of our grade! When are you going to do it?"

"I'll get it done, Mother!"

"You better be careful. . . . What if your mom finds out you're drinking?"

"Honestly, Lins! When you die, I'm going to personally carve on your tombstone. I'm going to write, 'Here lies Lindsey Anna Marshall. She died of worry, and for naught, because alas, her mother *never did find out!*'"

"Very funny. I'll see you later." As Lindsey hung up, she was more than a little concerned. Nearly all of her friends drank, but lately it seemed that Holly didn't know how to have a good time without alcohol. And now, she was drinking in the middle of the day. It just wasn't right. It wasn't like Holly at all. . . .

"Lindsey's not coming. She's gotta work on her science project," Holly told Billy.

"Aw, that's too bad."

"She's getting to be a drag lately. She got all hacked off because you and I had one little swig behind the snack shack yesterday." Holly got some glasses from the bar and a can of cola. "Well, I guess it's just you and me, Bud. Wanna play some cards?"

"Sure."

They played for a long time, laughing and talking between games of "Go Fish."

Holly won three games in a row.

"I swear, you cheat, Holly! I know you had some fours and you didn't give them to me."

She was high from the alcohol and felt silly. She wrinkled up her nose. "I know you had some fours and you didn't give them to me," she mimicked.

He picked up a pillow and hit her over the head. Soon, they were wrestling on the couch. She pinned him down and began digging her knuckles into his ribs until he was laughing hysterically. "Cut it out!" he pleaded, struggling until he got free.

He knocked her over and pretended to smother her with a pillow. She got up, grabbed his ankle and pulled off his shoe, tickling the bottom of his foot while he laughed and squirmed from discomfort.

They laughed and giggled until they both collapsed, exhausted, on the floor. They stared up at the ceiling in silence, each breathing hard from the strenuous wrestling match.

"Man alive!" Billy said. "You should go out for the team."

"I don't like the outfits." She rolled over on her side and propped herself up on her elbow. "You know, Billy, you're the best friend I have. You're so dependable . . . so thoughtful. . . . I really appreciate your coming over today. I appreciate the flower, and I appreciate the rum—especially the rum!" she giggled.

He rolled over and kissed her sweetly on the cheek. "I love you, Holly. I love you more than anyone."

She wasn't surprised at all by the remark. She knew Billy loved her, but it wasn't a romantic love. The love he had for her was different. It went deeper—and it had lasted longer.

Billy's love wasn't dependent on Holly doing anything or being any special way. His love was just there . . . all the time. Holly could always depend on it. *Billy really loves me,* Holly thought, *more than he loves himself.*

"Hey, Billy, would you take me to the dance Saturday night?"

He sounded shocked. "Homecoming? You want *me* to take you?"

"No, I want your uncle Ned. Yes, I want *you* to take me! You're my best boy-type friend. We'll have a blast! You want to?"

He smiled. "Yeah. I do want to!"

Holly's light was still on when her mom got home, so she knocked softly on the door. "Can I come in?"

"It's open."

Holly was lying on her bed, staring at the ceiling. She'd had too much to drink and had fallen asleep after Billy left. Now, she was wide awake and feeling woozy.

"You look pale. Do you feel all right? Why are you sleeping with your clothes on? Are you sick?" When Holly's mom sat down beside her, she thought she smelled liquor. When she bent down to kiss her daughter, she was sure of it.

"Holly, have you been drinking?"

"Me? Of course not!"

"Don't lie to me, Holly. I can smell it!"

She lay still, not sure of what to say. "Okay. I had a sip to celebrate my princess-hoodness," she giggled.

"I'd say you had more than a sip!"

"Well, I sipped it from a gallon jug."

"That's *not* funny!"

"I'm going to be sick!" Holly jumped off the bed and ran into the bathroom.

When she came back, her mother was pacing the floor beside her bed. "You made a bad choice for yourself here, Holly."

"Says who?" She plopped down on the bed.

"Says *me*, smart aleck! Whatever possessed you to get drunk?"

"I told you, I was celebrating!"

"Who with?"

"Not with *you*, that's for sure. You're too busy!"

"Oh, is that what this is all about?"

Holly ran into the bathroom again, this time only making it to the sink. When she finished throwing up, her mom was standing in the doorway.

"Go lie down. I'll bring you a cool rag for your head."

She dabbed the cold washcloth against Holly's forehead and around her temples.

"My head hurts so bad."

"Good. You want some aspirin?"

"I don't think I could keep it down."

"Holly, I'm sorry about this afternoon. I wish I could get out of my speaking engagement and take you shopping tomorrow, but I just can't. I thought you'd understand."

"I thought *you'd* understand!"

"Holly, that's not fair!"

She sat up, propping her pillow against the wall. "Mom, can't you remember what it was like to be a kid? Didn't you ever accomplish something special?"

"Well, of course I did."

"And what did Grandma Rachel do?"

She smiled at the recollection. "She made me a special cake. Chocolate with mint frosting in the center and covered with whipped cream! She used my play dishes—aluminum pans that you could put in a real oven—to make a special little cake just for me. Even when I was your age, she still made the same little cake in the same little pans!

"I can still see the look of pride on her face when I'd come home and tell her some wonderful thing I'd done. Once, when I was seven, I won a spelling bee. I came racing into the house after school, and there she was waiting . . ." she stopped mid-sentence, suddenly sensitive to the needs of her daughter. "That's it, isn't it? You're upset because I wasn't here for you when you came home from school!"

Holly began to cry. "I was so happy, and when I called you at the station, it was like you were just too busy to be bothered."

"Oh, baby!" She took Holly in her arms and held her close. "I'm so sorry. I've just been so busy with everything else lately. I *am* proud of you! You're the

116

most important thing to me, but this job is important, too! I've worked hard for this all of my life. I *have* to do my best! An opportunity like this will probably never come again. If I do well, my show could go national. That means people would be listening to me from California to New York!"

Holly thought it ironic that people would be listening to her mother from coast to coast, but her mother wasn't hearing a word *she* said, and they were right in the same room.

CHAPTER EIGHT

Holly's father stood with his camera raised. "Are you guys ready?"

"Oh, wait a minute, honey," his wife said. She took a tissue from the drawer and handed it to Billy. "You've got a spot on your face, right under your nose."

"Mom, I'm sure!" Holly protested.

"Well, I'm sure he'd rather wipe it off than have it in the picture."

Billy dabbed the tissue under his nose. "I had a nosebleed on the way over," he explained without embarrassment. "There, is it gone?"

"Perfect, now smile!" They both blinked from the flash.

"You look beautiful," Holly's dad said. "The dress is perfect."

She twirled around, the soft pink satin spinning in a graceful circle. The dress was unpretentious and elegant. Simple pearl earrings and a pink baby-rose wrist corsage were all the adornment she needed.

"I love the corsage, Billy. It's just perfect."

"I didn't know if I should get a wrist corsage or the kind you pin on. . . ."

"Oh, the wrist corsage is much better," Holly's mom offered. "That way, the flowers don't get smushed when you dance."

Holly had added more curl than usual to her hair and pulled one side of the ash-blonde tresses behind her ear, securing it with a tiny pink rosebud and white baby's-breath. She had redone her makeup twice. The first time, she tried some new eyeshadow and decided it looked too theatrical. Her makeup ended up the same as always, but tonight she had a special glow that couldn't have been achieved by even the greatest makeup artist.

They posed in front of the fireplace for one final picture.

"I've never seen a more handsome couple," Holly's mom said.

❖ ❖ ❖

The theme for the homecoming dance was "Evening in Paradise," and as chairperson of the decorating committee, Heidi Wagner had done a spectacular job in transforming the gym into a tropical utopia.

Students from the art department had painted a mural on the south wall. It showed the ocean with waves crashing against rocks and sea gulls soaring against a sun-streaked sky. There were swaying palm trees and sandy beaches with footprints leading into the sea. Paper orchids decorated the tables, and tropical birds—formed meticulously from papier mâché—were perched in rented palm trees. The trees were lit with hundreds of miniature twinkle-lights and were placed randomly throughout the gym.

Willie Boyd's Rock Boys—dressed in white dinner jackets with red carnations in their buttonholes—played live music on the stage, as most of the kids from Kennedy High slow-danced to the sultry sound of Willie's saxophone.

Billy's tuxedo was black, and he wore a red cummerbund that matched his bow tie. His dark hair had been cut earlier that day, and now each hair was meticulously placed.

Billy stood a good two inches above Holly, even though she had on high-heels. If he did say so himself, they made one good-looking couple. He smiled, confident that she was pleased as well.

"I'm having a great time," she said. "And you look terrific!"

Billy blushed. He'd never worn a tuxedo before. He felt like a mannequin in a department store window.

Holly scrutinized him carefully. "You know, I never realized how handsome you are."

"I've been telling you that ever since that day at the petting zoo!" he joked.

Her rhinestone tiara kept slipping, and she giggled as she pushed it back onto the top of her head. "I wouldn't make very good royalty." She felt a little embarrassed.

Billy held her close as they danced. "You'd make a good anything," he said sincerely.

The music stopped, and before another song began, Jeff was standing next to Billy. "Can I dance with your girl?" he asked politely.

"Sure."

Jeff didn't see the anger on Cindy's face as she turned and stomped into the rest room.

Jeff put his arm around Holly, and they began to dance. He couldn't take his eyes off of her. Jeff thought she was about the prettiest girl he had ever seen. He swallowed hard before he spoke. "You look beautiful . . . really beautiful. I envy your date. I wish you were with me tonight."

She feared he could hear her heart thumping. "Thank you. Are you having a nice time?"

"Actually, I had more fun at my Uncle Bob's funeral." She knew he was teasing. "Cindy can't accept the fact that she didn't win, and she's dedicated the rest of her life to making everyone pay for it. Don't drink the paradise punch. I think she put arsenic in it to punish everyone who didn't vote for her."

Holly laughed. "Well, it's too bad she didn't win. I know it meant a lot to her," she said sympathetically.

"I wish you were my date," he said again, holding her tighter.

She relaxed in his arms as he led her gracefully around the dance floor. Holly felt wonderful when she was with Jeff. He had something special—something that set him apart from other boys she knew. Jeff was gentle and self-assured. He was . . . different.

She closed her eyes and thought back to the night of Ryan's party and the things that she and Jeff had talked about. She'd thought often about that conversation. She remembered what Jeff had said about Jesus. She wanted to ask him to say more, but she knew this wasn't the right time.

122

The dance was over, and they both felt awkward. "Thank you," she said.

He bowed deeply at the waist. "Thank *you*, princess."

"You're welcome."

Billy was waiting expectantly at the table as Holly seemed to float toward him. "You really like that guy, don't you?"

She kissed him on the cheek. "Yeah, I really do," she said dreamily. Then she added quickly, "But you're still the cutest guy here! Hey, Billy, I have to go to the rest room. I'll be right back."

Once inside the bathroom, she found herself standing face to face with Cindy Aldrich. Holly's heart began to pound, and she felt the lump in her throat swell until she thought she wouldn't be able to speak. She swallowed hard. "Hi, Cindy."

"Well, if it isn't the little *princess*," she spat. "My, don't you look *sweet!* You look so sweet I think I'd like to puke!"

"Well, I'm sorry you feel that way. Excuse me." Holly attempted to walk around her, but Cindy stepped sideways, blocking her path. Holly looked nervously for support, but there was no one there except the two of them.

"Where do you think you're going?"

"I thought I'd go to the bathroom, if that's all right with you?"

"Nothing you do is all right with me!"

Holly tried to keep the fear from her voice. "As I said, I'm sorry you feel that way."

When Holly attempted to walk around her again, Cindy reached over and yanked the tiara off the top of her head, taking with it a clump of Holly's hair. Holly screamed out in pain. And before she could stop her, Cindy ran into a stall and threw the rhinestone crown into the toilet.

Instinctively, Holly took Cindy by the arm and yanked her out of the stall. Then she lifted the hem of her dress and bent over to retrieve her crown. As she reached her hand into the water, Cindy kicked Holly's backside, pushing her violently toward the toilet. Holly caught her balance just in time to keep her head from crashing against the wall. She was outraged! She spun around, losing all control of her tongue. "You're *pathetic*! You may be pretty on the outside, but inside you're the ugliest, meanest person I've ever known! I despise you!"

Holly's wet, gloved hand hung loosely at her side with the rhinestone crown dangling from her fingertips. A soggy glob of hair hung from the tiara, dripping water onto her dress. Her hair was lopsided, and her corsage rested sideways on her wrist.

Cindy burst out laughing. "You call *me* pathetic? Look at yourself!"

Holly peered past her into the mirror. Then, she broke down in sobs. "I hate you! You ruined *everything*!"

"Not quite," she said, digging in her purse. Then, very coolly, she waved Jeff's class ring in front of Holly's nose and asked, "When you were dancing with Jeff a while ago, did he happen to mention that we're going steady again? *So stay away from him!*"

Cindy was out the door like a bullet.

Holly sank onto a chair. She couldn't believe it: *He went back with Cindy!* She wanted to die.

❖ ❖ ❖

Holly pulled Billy away from the others and told him what had happened. As always, he was more than generous with his sympathy. He listened for a long time, thinking of things he'd like to do to fix Cindy's high and mighty wagon. But all he did was think about it. He never would have actually done anything to Cindy, because he knew Holly wouldn't approve. Finally, he said, "I'm sorry, Hol. I know you really like him. But you could have about any guy in the world!"

"That's what you say because you're my friend," she said sadly. "Jeff's the only guy I want . . . and *she's* got him! I just don't understand it. I thought he really liked me."

"He's gotta be nuts to throw you over for her!" He shook his head slowly, unable to figure the whole thing out. "It sure doesn't make any sense to me. Well," he said thoughtfully, "maybe if he thinks you like someone else, he'll come to his senses."

He gave her a kiss. "Cheer up, princess, this is *your* night. Don't let anything spoil it for you. Let's go have some fun!" He grabbed her hand and pulled her from her chair.

She smiled and threw her arms around him. She ached inside, but she was practical enough to realize that nights like this one were few and far between. For now, at least, she was going to try not to worry about it. . . . "You're right. No one's gonna spoil this! I've got all you guys. Let's party!"

Billy and Holly shared some champagne in the parking lot and then went back inside to the dance. Kevin and Sandy were engaged in a loud, heated argument when they got back to their table.

"I swear," Billy teased, "if you two ever get married, you'll give new meaning to the words 'domestic unrest.'"

Sandy ignored him. "Holly, you want to go to the ladies' room?" she asked angrily.

"No thanks, I've been there." She shot a knowing smile at Billy.

"Then come with me to get some punch. I gotta get away from here for a minute."

When the girls were out of earshot, Kevin said, "I don't know what's wrong with her. She's convinced that I'm seeing someone else. No matter what I say, she refuses to believe me."

"Are you seeing someone else?"

"Of course not. She'd kill me!"

"Don't worry about it then. She'll cool off." Billy tapped the bottle inside his coat. "Let's go outside."

Holly, Sandy, and Lindsey were ogling each other's dresses when Billy, Kevin, and Dave came back into the gym-turned-paradise.

"Where have you been?" Sandy asked.

Kevin walked closer, staggering slightly. She knew immediately where he'd been.

"Oh, I get it," she said.

"Billy's got another bottle in the van. You girls want to come outside?" he whispered.

Holly turned to the others. "Why not?"

"We might as well," Sandy said.

Reluctantly, Lindsey followed.

They sat on the floor in Billy's van, passing the bottle along with stories and laughter. They drank quickly, afraid they might be missed, and maybe one of the chaperones would come looking for them.

"If I couldn't win princess, I'm glad you did," Sandy said after a while.

"Thanks, Sands!" Holly put one arm around Sandy and the other around Lindsey and squeezed them both. "As far as I'm concerned, we *all* should have won. Boy, this is the greatest! . . . The best day of my life and my best friends to share it with me!"

She took another drink, and suddenly, she had tears in her eyes. "My mom and dad didn't even care about my being a princess. . . ."

"That's not true," Lindsey said. "They care!"

"No they don't. All they care about is their stupid jobs. And Jeff went back with Cindy."

"*No!*" Lindsey said, "I don't believe it!"

"Believe it. I ran into her in the rest room, and she waved his class ring in my face like she was trying to cast a hypnotic spell on me or something!"

She changed the subject and slumped against the window. Her tiara was all askew, and her bottom lip protruded like a pouting child's. "My mom used to care about everything I did. Now she's too busy listening to everyone else's problems to care about me!"

Billy cracked open another bottle of vodka. Lindsey watched uncomfortably as they continued to drink.

Sandy took a bag of peanuts out of her purse and passed them around, skipping Billy. "You don't get any because you didn't eat your dinner!" she scolded.

"Yeah," Holly said, "I can't believe you wasted that whole steak."

"I wasn't hungry."

127

"Well, okay, you can have some peanuts. . . ."

"No thanks, I'm not hungry."

Everyone was getting loud, and Dave and Kevin were beginning to act obnoxious. Lindsey wished she'd come with Matt instead of Dave. Though Lindsey loved Holly, sometimes she felt like she didn't belong with these kids at all.

"Parents are a bummer," Billy said.

Holly agreed, but she couldn't worry about that now—she was a princess! The most popular girl in the sophomore class. This was definitely the best day of her life.

Billy passed her the bottle again, and she took another sip. "Thanks, Billy."

"It's the least I can do for a princess."

She laughed, offering the bottle to Lindsey.

"No thanks, I've had enough."

Dave grabbed it and shoved it under her nose. "Have another sip!"

"I don't want any more!" She said, pushing it away.

"My, aren't we testy?" Sandy teased.

"I'm not testy!" Lindsey protested. "I just don't want any more to drink!"

Holly wrinkled her nose and looked squint-eyed at Lindsey, as she smoothed her pink satin dress so it wouldn't wrinkle before the pictures. "What's wrong, Lins?" she said, slurring her words so that it sounded like "Wash runglins?"

"Nothing's wrong," she said flatly.

"Well, somethin's wrong," Sandy persisted. "You just chewed my head off!"

Lindsey kept silent. She knew that there was

128

nothing she could say without offending them.

Sandy grabbed the vodka and took a long swallow.

It was so quiet, Lindsey could hear her watch ticking.

"What time is it?" Holly asked.

"Nine-forty-five."

"Ohmagosh," she said, grabbing at her tiara, "ish almosh time for pishers!"

Understandably, Brenda was the center of attention. Cindy spent the whole evening next to her, because it made good sense to at least be seen with the homecoming queen. If the truth be told, Cindy had never hated anyone more than she hated Brenda at that moment. As far as Cindy was concerned, Brenda was wearing *her* crown.

She nudged Brenda with her elbow, almost knocking her off her chair. "Smile, stupid, he's taking our picture again."

Brenda looked blankly into the camera.

Cindy smiled sweetly at the photographer. "My name's Cindy Aldrich. I was a finalist for queen. . . ."

"I'll make a note of it."

"Jeff," Cindy whined, "I'm so-o-o thirsty. Would you be sweet and get me some punch?"

Once he was gone, she bent across the table and said to the girls, "Honestly, he follows me around like a puppy. . . . So, Brenda, are you going to do it or not?

Brenda didn't hesitate. "No! I told you 'no,' and I meant it!"

"Just *do* it. It's only a joke! Who can it hurt?"

Brenda knew very well who it could hurt and so did Cindy. "Why don't *you* do it?"

129

"Because I won't be on the platform . . . *you* will!"

Brenda looked at Cindy and then at the others. They all expected her to do it, just because Cindy told her to. Everyone always did everything Cindy told them to.

"Go ahead," Rachel urged. "She deserves it. It's her fault Cindy lost."

"No one deserves that!" Brenda said. "And it's not her fault!"

Cindy grabbed her arm, squeezing until it hurt. "Listen to me, Brenda. You better do it or *else!*"

That was it. Brenda had had enough. *She* was the queen, not Cindy. And she was through taking orders.

She yanked her arm free. "Or else *what?*"

Cindy stammered, "Or else . . . or else you're out of the group!"

"Says *who?*"

Cindy looked to the others for support, but there was none. The girls were confused. Cindy had always been the leader, but everyone knew the homecoming queen was the most popular girl in school. . . .

Brenda looked directly at Rachel. "Holly Henderson is *not* the reason Cindy lost! Cindy lost because everyone's tired of her and of her mean, conniving ways of getting what she wants . . . no matter who she hurts! Holly's never done *anything* to me, and if you think I'm going to trip her in front of all these people, you better think again! It's the meanest, most heartless thing I can imagine. If you guys do anything like that, you'll have to do it without me! Now, if you'll excuse me, I have . . ." she spit the words in Cindy's face, "*homecoming queen pictures!*"

130

Cindy slouched into her chair, humiliated beyond comprehension. If she'd had a voodoo doll, the pins would have gone into Brenda's heart.

The other girls sat in silence, each afraid to speak for fear of suffering Cindy's wrath.

Suddenly, a sly smile crossed her lips, and she jumped up from her chair: *Rachel! Rachel Warner was senior princess!* She turned to Rachel who was seated across from her. "Rachel, *you* do it!"

The spotlight was on the stage as the school principal began calling the names of the homecoming queen and her court.

Holly was feeling dizzy, partly from the alcohol and partly from the excitement. "Those schteps look awfully intimidating," she said in a slurred mumble.

Billy was confident. "Just hold onto my arm."

"I think I drank too much. . . . I feel dizzy."

All of a sudden, the spotlight was shining on her as she heard Mr. Wallace's voice over the loudspeaker: "And from the sophomore class, Princess Holly Henderson!"

Her knees grew weak while cheering voices encouraged her to take her place on the platform. She heard "o-o-oohs" and "ah-h-h-s" of approval as the other girls admired her dress.

As Billy led her up the steps, the room began to spin around her. She wished she would have quit drinking sooner. Taking slow, deep breaths, she prayed she wouldn't pass out. Finally, she reached the top of the steps and turned to face the audience below.

The first face she saw was Jeff's. He was smiling warmly, and he winked at her. Cindy was behind him and seemed to be arguing with Rachel about some-

131

thing. Jeff thought Holly looked nervous, so he gave her a "thumbs up" for encouragement. *Always Mr. Nice Guy,* Holly thought.

Miss Connors handed Holly long-stemmed red roses just as Mr. Wallace called the name of the junior princess: "Gail Colvin!" Cheers rang out again as Gail made her way up the steps. She was followed by Rachel Warner, the senior princess, and finally, by Brenda Melroy, the queen.

Once all of the girls had their flowers, the lights were turned up and a team of photographers began snapping pictures from every angle. The queen and her court smiled widely as flashbulbs exploded amid loud cheers and whistles from an admiring crowd of their peers. Music pulsated through the auditorium as the Rock Boys played songs fit for teen royalty.

All the nervousness left her, as Holly was lifted past reality into a world only dreamed of by most. Every girl in the audience envied her presence on the platform. Holly Henderson knew there could be no feeling more special than this. For these brief moments, she was the pearl in the oyster. She wished the feeling could last forever.

Mr. Wallace announced the traditional "Queen's Waltz" as Brenda and her escort led the way down the steps onto the dance floor.

Billy noticed Rachel eyeing Holly nervously. Holly noticed it, too. "Is my schlip showing?" she whispered to Billy.

He looked behind her. "No."

She spoke through a beauty-pageant smile, "Is there spinish in my teeth?"

132

He scrutinized her pearly smile. "No," he laughed. "No spinach."

"What's she schtaring at, then? Huh?"

"She wants me," he deadpanned.

Holly looked at Rachel as if to ask, "What's wrong?" but Rachel quickly looked the other way.

The court and their escorts stood poised on the platform until Brenda's dance was finished. Then, the four princesses and their escorts were to join her for a second dance.

The senior princess had been instructed to leave the platform first, but Rachel didn't move. She was trying to get up her nerve. . . . She couldn't believe she was even considering what Cindy had suggested. . . . Finally, Gail left in her place.

Holly was waiting for Rachel, but Rachel motioned for her to go ahead. Holly nudged Billy. "Let's go!" she whispered.

He pulled back, waiting cautiously for Rachel. "We're supposed to wait. Rachel was supposed to go before Gail!"

"I know, but she motioned for *us* to go. I don't know what's wrong. Let's just go," she whispered.

As Billy and Holly tried to decide what to do, Jane Cullity, the freshman princess, left the platform, leaving only Holly, Rachel, and their escorts.

When Rachel didn't move, Holly pulled on Billy's arm, forcing him to lose his balance. "Come on, mallet head!" she joked, pulling him toward the steps.

He saw Rachel's foot just as she extended it in front of Holly. With the gracefulness of a swan and the quickness of a bullet, Billy caught Rachel's foot with his and

133

gave it a hardy jerk, sending her crashing to the floor of the platform. Before anyone knew what had happened, he was helping her to her feet.

"Oh my gosh, Rachel! Are you all right?" he asked with mock concern.

Her face ablaze with embarrassment, she stared at the ocean of puzzled faces, all abuzz with the news of what had happened. Concern mixed with ripples of laughter as word of her clumsiness spread all the way to the back of the gym. She yanked free of his hand. "I'm just *fine*, thank you! Next time, keep your big feet out of the way!"

"Same to you," he said.

He took Holly's hand and escorted her carefully down the stairs. "Be careful," he cautioned. "Watch your step."

Holly shuffled slowly and deliberately behind him, squinting at the floor as it appeared to move beneath her feet. When she was safely on the dance floor, she breathed a sigh of relief. She was feeling really woozy. She took a deep breath, screwed up her face, and said, "I feel sick."

She was weaving. All the color had left her face, and her mouth hung open. Billy put his hand under her chin and gently pushed her jaw shut. "Flies might get in there."

"Everything's spinning. . . . I feel s-s-sick!"

Holly didn't notice Cindy standing beside her until the sarcasm in her voice cut Holly like a dull razor. "What's that I heard? You're *sick*?"

She came closer, and Billy jumped between them, offering his body as a shield against the enemy. "She's got the flu," he lied.

134

Cindy feigned sympathy. "The *flu*? Gee, that's funny . . . she was fine earlier this evening." She strained to see past Billy and get a better look at Holly. "You sure it's the flu?"

"Yeah. Pretty sure." In a flash, Cindy was on the platform with the microphone in her hand. She tapped it hard with her fingers. The crowd groaned as a high-pitched squeal amplified throughout the gymnasium. She spoke loudly, "Testing. Testing."

When she had the attention of everyone on the dance floor, she cooed softly into the microphone. "Hi. Is everyone having a good time?"

Loud cheers and piercing whistles of approval rose from the crowd.

"Great. I'm having a good time, too. Listen, before we have the dance of the queen's court, there's someone here who would like to say a few words of gratitude to those of you who voted her sophomore princess. Please welcome *Holly Henderson!*"

The applause was instantaneous as the most popular girl in the sophomore class struggled to maintain her composure. She shot a puzzled look at Billy.

A drum roll swelled, increasing the anticipation, as a bright spotlight searched the dance floor and came to rest on Holly. Lifting her arm, she attempted to shield her eyes from the glare. She forced a smile and peered into the crowd.

"What'll I do?" she asked desperately. The light was suffocating. She felt as if she was going to faint.

"You have to go. She's already announced you. Just say a few words, thank everyone, and we're home free." Billy wrapped her arm through his and began to lead her slowly back up the steps. "Just hang on to me," he said confidently.

There were gasps of astonishment mixed with laughter as Holly tripped on the stairs and fell to her knees. Billy helped her up. "Are you all right? Did you hurt yourself?" he whispered.

"No, I'm okay," she said, straightening her tiara.

When they reached the platform, she took a deep breath and turned toward the crowd.

Cindy slapped the microphone into Holly's hand. "Let's see you get out of *this*," she seethed. She smiled sweetly to the crowd and walked gracefully down the steps, leaving Holly completely dumbfounded.

The applause turned to silence as Holly's friends waited eagerly to hear what she had to say. She stared into the crowd, her mind blank. Billy nudged her, and she rubbed her head where the tiara was pulling on her hair. She forced a dumb smile. Everyone flinched as she yelled "*Hi!*" at the top of her lungs into the microphone. "Thish ish really. . . ."

She swayed, and Billy was afraid she was going to pass out. He moved closer and took hold of her hand. "Go ahead," he prodded, "say something."

She put her fingers to her lips and giggled. "Billy wants meda schpeak. Soooo, I'm schpeaking!"

An explosion of moaning and laughter filled the gym as everyone realized, in unison, that Holly Henderson was drunk. She felt a tug on her arm as Billy tried to pull her away from the front of the stage.

"Wait!" she shouted, "I'm not through yet!"

Willie Boyd attempted to save the evening as the sound of his saxophone billowed out over the laughter.

136

His guitar player yanked the mike from Holly's hand, "Go get some air. You're *wasted*," he said gruffly. Then he turned to the crowd. "Everybody dance!" he commanded.

"Did you see that?" she slurred. "He pulled that right outta my hand!"

"Yeah, I saw it," Billy said calmly. "He's afraid you're gonna steal his gig."

Holly began to cry. "No he's not! He says I'm wa-a-asted," she whined.

Holly resisted as Billy attempted to lead her down the steps. "Come on, Hol. You're just gonna make things worse!" Reluctantly, she followed, almost losing her balance again on the way down.

Cindy waited victoriously at the bottom of the steps. "Nicely done, your royal high*nish*."

Laughter engulfed the gym, swallowing Holly like a cold and treacherous wave. In that instant, the comments of the crowd forced her into the depths of despair.

"She's smashed!"

"Nice speecsh, prinshess."

"Look at her, she can hardly walk!"

Lindsey pushed her way through the crowd. If Holly ever needed a friend, it was now. She put an understanding hand on Holly's arm. "Let's go outside, Hol."

Holly jerked her arm free. "Leeme alone!"

Lindsey felt as if her heart had been pierced. "Holly, I. . . . Oh, never mind!" She started to cry.

Holly looked past Lindsey and saw Jeff. Immediately, she started toward him. She wanted to explain everything. "Jeff, I. . . ." But the look on Jeff's face told her not to bother.

"Come on, Billy. Lesh get outta here! Who needs this, anyway?"

When they were safely outside, the reality of what had happened hit her, and Holly collapsed into Billy's arms. She buried her head in his chest. "Oh, Billy," she sobbed, "I'm so humiliated! I wish I was dead!"

She heard footsteps and looked up to see Dave, Sandy, and Kevin running toward her. Sandy rushed to her side and knelt down beside her. "Wow, I didn't realize you had so much to drink!"

"You're right, Hol, who needs 'em, anyway?" Dave offered.

Lindsey stood back, alone, listening. She was completely amazed that they could take it all so casually. She felt genuinely mortified for Holly and afraid that the best friend she had ever known had slipped away forever.

❖ ❖ ❖

It was too much for Holly to expect her mom and dad to be up when she got home. It was just as well, she reasoned. She couldn't bear to have them see her like this.

She stood in front of her bedroom mirror, looking with disgust at her reflection. How could she have allowed this to happen on the best night of her life?

She was grateful that Billy had been thoughtful enough to stop by to see his "supplier" and pick up a bottle of cherry brandy on the way home. After a couple of drinks, the whole incident didn't seem so bad. Before long, they were laughing about it.

She put on her nightgown and climbed under the

covers. It was then, when she was all alone in the quiet darkness, that the gravity of the entire situation hit her like a blow to the head. She thought about all those kids laughing at her and calling her names. Then, she thought of Jeff. If there was ever a chance that she could get him back, she'd blown it for good now. He'd probably never even speak to her again. She'd ruined everything.

She rolled over on her side, burying her head underneath her pillow. Her eyes filled with tears as she moaned, "Oh, God, what have I done?"

CHAPTER NINE

When Lindsey arrived at school on Monday morning, Cindy, Rachel, and Sandy were engaged in loud, animated conversation next to the lockers. They suddenly stopped talking when they saw her coming.

Lindsey looked at Sandy, curious to know the secret.

"I'll talk to you later," Sandy told Cindy. "Meet me after school."

Cindy walked slowly past Lindsey as she stood by her locker. "Where's your faithful sidekick, her royal highnish?" she mocked.

"If you mean Holly, I guess she's gonna be late this morning."

"Well, don't worry about it. She's probably just hung over."

Lindsey slammed the locker shut, angry at Holly for shutting her out. She'd called twice on Sunday, and Holly wouldn't even talk to her. Lindsey wanted Holly to know that she was sticking by her, no matter what.

It hurt her that Holly wouldn't give her a chance to show that she understood.

There was no way Lindsey could have known that Holly longed to be with her, to cry on her shoulder and tell her how miserable she felt. But Holly was certain that even Lindsey wouldn't want to associate with her anymore. She wanted to save Lindsey the embarrassment of having to tell her so.

When Lindsey got to the table at lunch, the other kids were already there, gathered around Holly.

They were laughing loudly. "I'll never forget it if I live to be a hundred," Dave was saying.

"Well, at least it wasn't *me* this time," Billy joked.

"Did you see Mr. Wallace?" Kevin asked. "I thought he was going to pass out!"

They all laughed uproariously at the recollection.

There was a note of sarcasm in Sandy's voice: "I thought he'd die when he realized his precious little cheerleader-princess was roaring drunk!"

Holly had thought about staying home from school, but she realized that the sooner she faced everyone, the sooner the whole thing would blow over.

She had prepared herself for the volley of jokes, sneers, and wisecracks that would be thrown at her all day. She'd seen it enough with Billy to know what to expect. So, when they all started in on her, she pretended not to care. At this point, she guessed it was better just to make a joke of it herself.

Lindsey tossed her lunch bag on the table. "I got roast beef today, Hol. You want half?"

Holly looked uncomfortable. "No thanks, Lins."

"You're not eating?"

"That's right."

The resentment was unspoken, but clear to Holly. She knew Lindsey was mad at her for getting drunk, and she wasn't about to give her the opportunity to tell her so.

Lindsey was about to speak when Doug Jetty approached their table. "How you feeling today?" he asked sincerely.

"A little less dignified than I was on Saturday. But other than that, I'm fine," Holly said.

"That's good," he said. "Wanna go out sometime?" It was as if by getting drunk and making a fool of herself, Holly had won Doug's respect. The fact that someone as crude and disgusting as Doug Jetty was now attracted to her only reaffirmed the contempt she felt for herself. He was standing over her, waiting for an answer, while all her friends choked back their laughter.

"Thanks," she said, "but I'm kind of . . . you know, seeing someone regularly."

"If you mean Jeffy Boy, I don't think you'll have ta worry about that."

Apparently, Cindy hadn't wasted any time in telling everyone that she and Jeff were back together. "Oh?" Holly said, feigning ignorance. "Why not?"

Doug snorted at her. "You gotta be kiddin'! You think a goody-two-shoes Jesus-freak like him'll date a chick who drinks like you?"

His statement jolted Holly like an electric shock and shamed her beyond imagination. Tears of humiliation flooded her eyes as she jumped up from the table and ran into the rest room, slamming the door behind her.

143

"You jerk!" Lindsey shouted at him. "Who asked for your opinion, anyway?" She ran after Holly.

When Lindsey got to the bathroom, she banged on the door of the stall Holly was in. "Come out, Holly. Let's talk! It's not so bad. . . . Please, Holly, come on out."

The sound of Holly's deep, wrenching sobs vibrated loudly off the tile walls and floor of the bathroom. Repeatedly, Lindsey pleaded with her to come out. But Holly refused to respond. There was nothing Holly Henderson—or anyone else—could say or do to make this situation go away.

❖ ❖ ❖

Everyone in school was talking about Holly that Monday, most of them seemingly aghast at the amount of embarrassment she had caused herself. It seemed that everywhere she turned, small clusters of kids—the same ones who had ogled and envied her at the beginning of the dance Saturday night—were now talking about her behind her back. She heard only parts of their muffled conversations:

". . . totally embarrassing!"

"I'd just *die* if I were her!"

"I never knew she drank like that."

". . . it was totally disgusting!"

As the day wore on, Holly sunk deeper and deeper into depression. She began counting the minutes until the day would be over. She just wanted to go home.

Finally, school was over for the day. But she still had cheerleading practice to contend with. For the first time in her life, she dreaded going to cheerleading practice. But there was only one week left until the regional finals . . . if she didn't show up, Miss Connors would have a fit!

Holly was on her way to her locker to get her pompoms when she saw Billy standing against the building. Though he was facing the wall, she could see that he had his hand over his face. As she walked closer, she saw blood oozing through his fingers.

She threw her books on the sidewalk and ran to him. "Billy! What's wrong?"

"It's just a nosebleed."

Now, the blood almost spurted through his fingers. It ran down his forearm and formed large droplets at the tip of his elbow before it hit the sidewalk.

"Just a nosebleed? My gosh, Billy, it's not *just* a nosebleed!" She ran into the bathroom and got some paper towels. "Here . . . now sit down and lean your head forward. Pinch your nostrils shut and breathe through your mouth."

She sat down next to him, watching the minute hand on her watch. "Stay like that until I tell you to move," she ordered.

Concerned, she waited five minutes and then told him he could put his head up. As soon as he did, the bleeding began again, so the process was repeated. Finally, it stopped.

"Where'd you learn that, *Nancy Nurse*?"

"I took first aid . . . for babysitting. Are you okay?"

"Sure. Thanks, Hol." When he stood up, he swooned. He felt like he was going to be sick to his stomach.

She jumped up, supporting him around the waist.

"Billy, you better go to the nurse."

He sat back down, resting his head on his knees. After a while, he smiled at her. "Whatever it was, it's passed. I feel better."

He had some color back in his cheeks, but his skin had a funny yellow cast to it.

He hugged her. "Thanks again, Hol. I gotta go."

She watched him walk away. She couldn't see him after he turned the corner and collapsed on the sidewalk behind the gym.

❖ ❖ ❖

When practice was finally over, Holly ached to go home and go to bed. She was totally exhausted. She grabbed her books and slammed her locker shut. When she turned around, Cindy and Rachel were standing behind her.

"You looked good in practice today," Cindy said.

"Thanks."

"You feeling a little better today?"

"Let's not play games, Cindy. What's on your mind?"

"What makes you think there's something on my mind, princess?"

Holly pushed past her. "Never mind. I gotta go."

"Tell me, Holly. Is it true what everyone's saying about you? Do you have a drinking problem?"

"Who said that?" Holly demanded.

"Well, actually, Jeff suggested it. . . . He wondered about you when you got drunk at Ryan's party, but he was sure of it after he heard your coronation speech . . . prinshess!"

"I don't believe you. Jeff never said that."

"Well," Cindy said, looking toward the gym, "here

146

he comes. Why don't you just *ask* him how he feels about dating a drunk? See you later." She swiped Holly in the face with a pom-pom.

Holly opened her locker quickly and pretended not to notice Jeff. She wanted to see if he'd come talk to her.

He walked directly over. "Hi."

She forced an embarrassed smile. "Hi."

He felt awkward. He didn't know what to say, but he felt he should say something. "You okay?"

"For a total fool, I guess I'm doing pretty well." She expected him to respond, to tell her it was all right, but he didn't. "I guess I blew it with you, didn't I?" she asked sadly.

He just looked at her, because he didn't know what to say. He liked her so much, and yet he knew they were just too different to be together.

"Jeff, I'm so sorry. I've learned my lesson. I'll never do anything like that again! I still want to go out with you. . . ."

He interrupted her, "I don't think it's a good idea for us to date anymore, Holly. I just don't think it'll work out."

"Sure it will!"

"No, it won't. We're too different."

Her emotions were tangled together like balls of old yarn. She felt embarrassment and remorse, but most of all, she felt hopelessness because there was nothing she could do to alter the situation she had created for herself. "I ruined *everything*," she cried. "Everything was perfect, and I ruined it all!"

"Why'd you do it, Holly?"

She studied him carefully. He'd already told her he

147

didn't want to date her anymore, so she had nothing to lose. "I did it because of you, because I felt so bad," she blurted out. "I did it because you went back with Cindy and didn't even have the courtesy to tell me! You made a fool out of me."

"What? Who told you I went back with Cindy?"

"*She* told me Saturday night. She did everything but hit me over the head with your stupid class ring!"

"Holly, I didn't go back with Cindy. She just wouldn't give my ring back until after homecoming." He held out his hand, showing his ring finger. "See?"

She looked at his hand. So, he didn't go back with Cindy. He *did* like Holly, after all. At least, he did until Saturday night. . . .

"I was so upset when she showed me the ring. I . . . I was stupid to get drunk like that."

"Well, listen, I gotta go. I'll see ya around, okay?" Jeff felt very awkward. He turned back to her. "Listen, Holly, I really like you. You're a great person. I want to be your friend, okay? There's no hard feelings. . . ."

"Sure, no hard feelings."

She watched him turn the corner and then sank to the floor against her locker. She was sobbing uncontrollably when Kevin found her.

"What's wrong, Holly?"

He sat down next to her and wrapped a sympathetic arm around her. She laid her head on his shoulder just as Sandy came around the corner.

She threw her notebook at him, hitting him near his shoulder. "So it's true!" she screamed.

"What's true?" Kevin asked, rubbing the sting from his arm.

148

She stood directly over Holly, her fists clenched tightly at her sides. "Cindy told me you were after him! I should have known. You lost Jeff and now you go after *my* boyfriend! I can't believe you'd do this, Holly!"

Holly jumped up. "Sandy, I. . . ."

"Never mind the explanations, Holly. Everything's perfectly clear!"

❖ ❖ ❖

Rounding the corner on his way to the parking lot, Jeff was shocked at the sight of Billy's body lying face down on the asphalt. He ran over and knelt down beside him.

Carefully, Jeff slipped his arm under Billy's chest and rolled him over. "Hey, buddy," he said quietly, "what happened?" He shook him gently. "Are you all right?"

Billy's head hung back loosely. He didn't open his eyes.

Jeff looked around helplessly. There was no one in sight. He took off his sweater, rolled it up, and placed it under Billy's neck. Then he began patting Billy's face until he opened his eyes.

He blinked, confused and disoriented. "Oh, man, I must've passed out." He tried to sit up, but Jeff held him back.

"Take it easy. Don't get up yet. Are you loaded again?"

"No. I haven't had a drink all day. I haven't been feeling too good lately."

"Well, you look like death warmed over. Sit up really slow and just stay put for a few minutes." Jeff

149

helped him sit up and sat down next to him.

"I'll be okay. You can go now."

"We'll just sit here a few minutes, and then I'll give you a lift home."

"I'm all right, really. You don't have to wait."

"I *want* to wait, okay?"

Billy was startled by Jeff's insistence. "Yeah, sure. Thanks." They sat silently for a few minutes, and then Billy said, "How long was I out?"

"I dunno. Not too long I guess, because someone would have found you. I must be the last one here. It's almost five-thirty. You been to a doctor?"

"Naw, I'm okay."

"No one's 'okay' who passes out for no apparent reason. You drink way too much. It's just not cool. You're on the wrong road, man!"

Billy ran his fingers through his hair. "Yeah? Well where's the right one?"

Jeff hesitated. He wanted to tell Billy that his drinking would lead nowhere, that he'd ruin his life. He wanted to tell him that even though Billy had a miserable life at home, there was hope. . . . "Jesus . . . I think Jesus is the right road," he said bluntly. He waited for a reaction, but there was none. "Listen, bud, just lay off the booze for a while before you kill yourself. And if you ever wanna talk—about anything—you call me, okay? I mean it." Jeff patted him warmly on the back. "Come on," he said, "I'll buy you a burger."

❖ ❖ ❖

"Hey, Holly, wait up!"

When Holly heard Lindsey's voice behind her, she

150

walked faster and pretended she didn't hear. Lindsey caught up with her anyway.

"That was some workout! I think we look great, though, don't you?"

"Yeah, I guess so."

"Miss Connors really thinks we're gonna win."

"Maybe. . . ."

"Did you see the picture of the trophies? They're huge!"

"We've got to get to Las Vegas first for the finals."

"I think we can do it!"

"Maybe. . . ."

"Holly, what's wrong with you?"

"Nothing."

"Well, something is. You haven't said two words to me all day. Did I do something?"

Holly's silence told Lindsey that she had.

She pulled on Holly's arm, forcing her to stop walking. "What did I do?"

"I . . . you . . . I know you're mad about Saturday night."

Lindsey thought about lying—telling Holly she wasn't mad—but they were too good of friends for that. "Okay, I guess I was mad. But I'm not mad anymore, honest. I'm just . . . worried."

"Worried about what?"

"Your attitude, I guess. You're changing, Holly— you're acting different. It bothers me . . . what happened Saturday night. You guys act like it's just a big joke. It wasn't funny, Holly. I'm worried about you. You drink too much." There, she'd finally said it.

"Me? You're crazy! I just like to have fun."

151

"Was making a total fool out of yourself in front of the whole student body your idea of fun?"

Holly was humiliated enough. She didn't need her best friend reminding her of what she'd done. "Who are you, my *mother*? What do you care what I do? Are you Miss Perfect or something? Yeah, that's you, all right—Miss Perfect! 'Don't sneak out, Holly. Your mom might find out.' 'Don't forget to do your science project, Holly.' 'Don't let your mom catch you drinking, Holly.' I get so *sick* of you sometimes!"

In all the years they had been friends, Holly and Lindsey had never had a fight. They went together like harmony and melody, like happiness and joy. . . .

"I'm sorry, Holly."

Holly started walking. "If you were really sorry, you'd stop judging me."

Lindsey couldn't believe the accusation. "I don't do that!"

"You *do* do it! I know you don't like it when I drink!"

"That's because you drink too much."

"I do not! I do *not* drink too much!" She began to cry, and she was almost running down the street.

Lindsey grabbed her arm. "Holly, please slow down! Let's talk. . . ."

"I don't want to talk!" She jerked her arm from Lindsey's grasp and glared at her. Then she watched as Lindsey's eyes filled with tears.

"Okay, Holly. If that's the way you want it."

She turned away, but Holly spun her around. "I'm sorry, Lins! Please stay. I need to talk to someone. Really. I'm sorry!"

They sat down on the curb. "Everything's a mess!

152

Jeff doesn't want to go out with me anymore, and it seems like everyone hates me. Cindy's making my life miserable. I'm nervous every day at school because I don't know what she's going to do to me next.

"I ruined my life Saturday night. I *have* to make a joke of it, because I can't stand to think seriously about how humiliating it was. Everyone in school thinks I'm a lush! And if all that isn't enough, Sandy thinks I'm trying to steal Kevin away from her."

"Sandy can't believe that!"

"Well, she does."

Lindsey was at a loss for words. Holly had created the situation, and there was no way to undo what had been done. Though Lindsey wanted more than anything to comfort her friend, she had no idea what to say.

Finally, she offered, "Well, things could always be worse. The Mescalero Indians used to strip their captives, stake them to sand dunes, and let the red ants eat them alive."

They both broke into laughter. "Oh, Lindsey, I love you so much!"

Billy was lying on his bed, thinking about what Jeff had said: "You're on the wrong road, man. . . . Jesus . . . Jesus is the right road."

He rubbed at his stomach, attempting to soothe the pain. He was consumed with an indescribable fear. He felt that something awful was going to happen. He felt desperate, but he didn't know why.

He took the tiny picture frame from his nightstand

153

and studied his mother's face. He missed her—not because of what she had been, but because of what he always wanted her to be. His eyes filled with tears as he thought of her in the hospital, dying.

If only he had someone. . . . If only there was someone who cared about him.

"Oh, Ma!" he cried out loud, "why couldn't things have been different?"

❖ ❖ ❖

Holly decided to stay up and wait for her mother to come home. She had a bottle of beer and worked on some extra credit for science. She was failing the class because she had neglected to turn in her science project. Mr. Hendricks told her he'd consider giving her a "D" if she showed some effort before the end of the quarter.

She heard her mother's car in the driveway and quickly buried the empty beer bottle in the trash can next to her desk. When she got downstairs, her mother was behind the bar, fixing herself a drink.

"Oh, hi, honey! How's my girl?"

"I'm fine." She ran over and threw her arms around her mother.

Holly's mom set her glass down and hugged her daughter tightly. "I don't know why you're doing this, but I like it!" She gave her a lot of little kisses. "Boy, I've missed your hugs, pumpkin!"

She released Holly and searched the bar for some vodka. "Gosh, can we be out of vodka?"

Holly became nervous. "There's got to be some there somewhere."

154

Holly's mom moved the bottles around. "No, I don't see any. There's hardly any rum, either. And we're out of wine!"

"You don't usually drink during the week."

"Well, I'd like a drink tonight, and we seem to be out of everything!"

"Why don't you just have a beer? I'll go get it for you."

"You know I don't like beer. What I really want is champagne," she said triumphantly. "Holly . . . they're giving me my own show!"

CHAPTER TEN

It was 3:15, and everyone was gathered around Holly's locker. Christine was raving mad. She threw her pom-poms down and grabbed Holly's arm. "I gotta talk to you!"

"What's wrong, Chris?"

"It's Billy. You have to talk to him, Holly. You're the only one he'll listen to. He was outside my house at 2:30 this morning—drunk and *crying*! He woke my mom and dad. I thought my dad was going to kill him! He was so drunk, I don't think he even knew where he was."

Lindsey ran over, tugging impatiently on Holly's shirt. "Holly! Billy got kicked out of school! Coach Sims found him drinking in the locker room again."

"Are you sure?"

"Kevin just told us."

"Oh my gosh," Holly said, chewing nervously on her nails, "his dad will kill him!"

The kids had broken into small groups, all of them waging guesses as to the severity of Billy's punishment once his dad found out he had been expelled.

The conversations stopped immediately when they saw Billy coming toward them.

He was unaware that they knew of his predicament. "Hey, gang!"

Kevin's voice was sad. "Hey, Billy."

"What's up? Who died?"

When no one spoke, he understood. "Oh, I get it. News travels fast around here. Yeah, it's true. I'm history in these hallowed halls." He turned to his locker, nervously fumbling with the combination lock. He tried it a couple of times and, unable to open it, pounded the cold steel in frustration.

"It's 35-15-4," Holly said slowly.

"What's gonna happen when you get home?" Kevin asked for all of them.

"Well, I don't know," Billy said, trying to make light of the situation, "but it won't be pretty." He finally got the locker open and began to empty it, tossing most of its contents into the trash can. He just wanted to get out of there before he started bawling like a baby.

He handed his algebra book to Holly. "Will you turn this in to old geezer-face for me tomorrow?"

"Sure, Billy."

He shut the locker and said, "Well, I'll see you guys in the funny papers!"

The kids encircled him, attempting to offer comfort. "We're sorry, Billy," Christine said.

"Hey listen, buddy. I could go home with you if you want . . . you know, when you tell your dad," Kevin offered.

Billy chuckled, patting his friend's shoulder. "Thanks, pal. But believe me, you don't want to be there."

158

"Billy, don't tell him!" Holly blurted. "Just don't tell him, and everything will be all right."

"No, it won't be all right," he said softly.

"You only got kicked out of *Kennedy*. You can still finish high school someplace else. . . . Just explain it to him," Holly said. "Really, Billy. It'll be okay."

He turned on her, his words stinging like a scorpion. "Why don't you just shut up? Whadda *you* know about 'okay'? Does your old man ever use you for a punching bag?"

"No, but. . . ."

"Then shut up, and leave me alone!"

Silence surrounded the group of kids like a thick, black cloud. Everyone knew what Billy's life was like, and no one wanted to trade with him.

Holly was crying, and Billy felt like a fool. He took her hand gently and looked into her eyes, seemingly unaware of the others watching. He curled his other hand around her neck and pulled her head onto his shoulder. He stroked her hair and kissed her tear-soaked cheek. "I'm sorry. I didn't mean it. You're the best pal I've got."

She sniffed back the tears. "I'm afraid for you," she said sincerely.

"I'll handle it," he promised. He forced a smile and addressed the group confidently. "Really, you guys, don't worry about me. I can handle this."

But everyone knew he couldn't.

❖ ❖ ❖

Billy was twenty minutes late, and Holly was beside herself with worry. She had reason to worry—she'd

159

seen Billy a couple of times after one of his father's beatings.

She sighed with relief when he finally came around the corner. He looked fine, and he was smiling.

"Wanna go get something to eat?" she offered.

"No thanks. I'm not hungry."

She scrutinized him carefully. "Are you losing weight? You look so thin."

He looked down at himself. "I dunno . . . maybe. I don't have any appetite lately. When I do eat, I can't keep anything down."

"I hope you're not getting that awful flu. . . . Well, what happened?" she asked anxiously.

"Nothing, I didn't tell him. He's never home anyway. He'll never know the difference." He pulled a flat bottle out of his hip pocket and took a drink. "I'm not going back to school. I decided to get a job. I'm failing most of my classes anyway. Wanna swig?"

She took the bottle and swallowed a sip. "What is this?" she asked, screwing up her face.

"Rye."

"It's sick!"

He laughed, playfully tweeking her nose.

"Are you sure you want to quit school?"

"Yeah. I'm gonna save some cash and blow this place. I think I'm headin' to Colorado." He got a faraway look in his eyes. "Holly, do you believe in God?"

"I don't know. I never really thought about it much. Do you?"

"Yeah." He looked up at the sky, squinting into the bright sunlight. "When I think of nature, it just blows me away . . . Rocky Mountains capped with snow, end-

160

less blue skys and bottomless oceans, animals, flowers, birds. . . .

"Did you know a hummingbird's wings move seventy times per *second*?" He shook his head, awed by the thought of it. "Someone really awesome created nature. There *has* to be a God."

"Do you go to church?"

"Naw."

"Me neither." She tipped the bottle up and winced as the dark brown rye burned its way into her stomach. "What do you think He looks like?"

"Who?"

She slugged him on the arm. "God, silly!"

"Oh, I dunno. Maybe He looks like Jesus. The Bible says Jesus is the image of God."

Her eyes widened. "You read the *Bible*?"

He was a little embarrassed. "Yeah," he said meekly, "sometimes. My grandma left it when she died."

She shook her head. "All this time I've known you, and I never even knew you read the Bible. . . . What else does the Bible say about God?"

He took another swig. "Are you serious?"

"Yes."

"Well, it says that God loves us no matter what we do."

"Do you believe that? That someone can love you even when you do really awful things?"

"If God says it, I believe it," he said flatly.

He took another long swallow and changed the subject. "You know, you're really the only friend I've got."

"Oh, that's not true."

"Yes it is. Everyone avoids me except you . . . and

161

Jeff. All the rest of 'em pretend to like me, but they talk behind my back. Even Kevin! Christine never liked me. She only dated me to make Dave jealous." He took another swig.

Holly pretended she didn't believe it, but Billy was right. All the kids talked about him behind his back. They said he acted like a fool and that he smelled bad. At first they thought it was funny, the way he got drunk and acted silly all the time. But as he did it more and more, the novelty wore off, and they merely grew tired of his antics.

"Billy, have you ever thought that maybe you drink too much?"

"No."

She hesitated, surprised by the flatness of his answer. "The last few months, I've hardly seen you sober."

"You've been keeping up with me pretty good! Besides, I feel better drunk."

She couldn't argue with that. Alcohol sure made her feel better lately. She remembered losing her embarrassment in a bottle of brandy after the dance.

He laughed out loud. "Hey, remember the time you glued my pants to the chair in art class?"

She laughed hard. "I didn't glue your pants to the chair! I accidentally spilled some glue, and you just happened to sit in it."

"'Accidentally,' my foot! I suppose it was pure coincidence that you 'spilled' it on *my* chair right after I told Marty you stuffed Kleenex in your bra!"

"Oh, too much!" she said, covering her face, "I forgot all about that! That was fifth grade. I thought I'd

162

die when you told him! I was so in love with Marty. . . . I only stuffed my bra because he kept looking at Ginger Melton."

"Good ol' Ginger," Billy said, remembering. "Boy, she was . . . built."

They laughed again. "I think that's the only time I was ever really mad at you."

"And boy, were you *mad!*"

They sat quietly, each comfortable in remembering. Holly never grew tired of Billy. He was the one person—even more than Lindsey—that she could be totally herself with. She could tell him anything, and she knew he would never judge her or betray her confidence. If she'd been lucky enough to have a brother, she would have wanted one as kind and loyal as Billy.

"Billy, are you lonely?" she asked finally.

He put his arm around her and pulled her close. "How could I be lonely with a pal like you? We stick together, you and me." He nudged her playfully.

"I'm serious. Sometimes I feel so lonely I could cry."

"That's ridiculous. You're the most popular girl in the sophomore class. How could you be lonely?"

"There are different kinds of loneliness."

"Somehow, I can't imagine anyone like you feeling lonely. . . ." He considered her question. When he finally answered, his voice was sad. "It's true what I said. You're the only friend I have. I guess I'm the loneliest person I know."

"Billy, do you think I drink too much?"

"You? No way! You just like to party."

Holly told him about the times she drank alone and about the Saturday night she got drunk while

163

her parents were out for dinner. "I didn't mean to get drunk," she confessed. "But the longer I sat there alone, the more I thought about how miserable I felt. I just kept drinking until I fell asleep."

"You're making too much out of it. There's nothing wrong with drinking a little too much sometimes. You just have to watch it so it doesn't become a habit."

"When I drink, I don't feel lonely anymore. I don't worry about things. . . ."

"What could someone like you possibly have to worry about?"

She had to admit that, next to Billy's life, hers was like a day at Disneyland. "The last few months, everything's caved in on me. On top of everything else, I'm failing two classes. If I don't get my grades up, I'll get kicked off the cheer squad!"

"Whoa! That *is* a bummer! What did your folks say?"

"I haven't told them. They probably wouldn't care anyway."

"*Your* folks? You gotta be kiddin'!"

"They used to care, but lately it seems like they don't even know I exist. I know they love me. They just don't have any time for me." She was picking blades of grass from the lawn and tossing them absent-mindedly into the autumn breeze. "It's as if they think I don't need them or something. . . . They're so wrapped up in their own lives, I feel like they don't even care what I do. And now that Mom's got her own show, that's all she talks about!

"My dad's the most insecure person I've ever met. He's so worried they're going to write him out of the show that he's almost unable to function. What's the big deal, anyway? It's just a TV show."

"Parents are a real bummer," Billy offered sympathetically.

"Oh, don't get me wrong. . . . I love my mom and dad. But lately, I feel like *I'm* the parent. I get caught sneaking out of the house and my mom tells me to punish myself. My dad calls me on the phone and dumps all his troubles on my shoulders. I cook my meals, clean the house, and lead my own life. . . . I could be married with children and they wouldn't notice!"

Billy took another swig of rye. "That's a bummer." All of a sudden, he doubled over in pain, grabbing his stomach. He was alarmingly pale.

Holly pushed him up. "Billy, what's wrong?"

"Cramps. I think I'm coming down with something. I've been feeling nauseated, and I can't keep anything in my stomach."

She looked at the near-empty pint of rye. "You shouldn't be drinking, then!" She grabbed the bottle and tossed it in the bushes.

He winced at the pain. "Oh, it hurts!"

Holly's mind raced. After Billy was expelled, she overheard a couple of the teachers talking about him. They were saying that Billy was an alcoholic. Holly never thought of him like that. Alcoholics were old men who wore dirty clothes and used street curbs for pillows. Alcoholics couldn't be *kids*, could they?

Then she recalled a conversation she'd had with Lindsey a few weeks before. "Billy drinks way too much," Lindsey had said. "If he doesn't quit, he'll kill himself one of these days."

165

It had seemed like a silly exaggeration at the time. But now, seeing him like this, Holly was stricken by the realization that maybe Lindsey—and the teachers—were right. He had been complaining of not feeling well lately, and he hadn't been eating either. She remembered the nosebleeds, and the dizziness he'd complained of. . . .

"Billy, you should see a doctor. There could be something really wrong with you!"

"You're entirely too dismal. It's just the flu."

"You don't have that kind of pain with the flu!" She rubbed his back. "Take some deep breaths."

He did, but that made the pain worse. He staggered off and stretched out on the grass.

"You should see a doctor," she repeated. "It's not just the flu, Billy. You look horrible. There's no color in your face!"

He just lay on the grass, trying not to show her how much it hurt. Suddenly, he thought of little Peter Hollis. "Holly, did you ever wonder what it would be like to be crippled? I mean, in a wheelchair and totally helpless?"

"No, why?"

"It would be awful, wouldn't it? Being a little kid, wanting to play with the others and knowing that no matter how badly you want it, you'll never be able to ride a bike or run a race." He was staring at the sky. "I think being crippled might even be worse than being dead."

Holly didn't understand why Billy was talking that way.

After a while he sat up. Slowly, the color came back

166

into his cheeks, and the pain subsided.

"Really, you should go see a doctor," she persisted.

"Will you relax? I'll be fine."

Somehow, she knew he wouldn't be.

Holly picked up the phone. "Hello."

"Hi. It's Dad."

"Hi, Daddy! How are things going?"

"Since you asked, they're not going well. They cut all my lines from Friday's script."

"But Friday's the most important day. That's when all the horrible stuff happens that doesn't get resolved until Monday. Everyone watches on Friday!"

"Yup."

"Oh, Daddy, that's terrible!"

"Well, it's not good, that's for sure. But since they did it, I'm taking Friday off. I'll take you and Mom out to eat Friday night."

"Okay!"

Holly poured a vodka over ice to get her through the boredom of her homework. After the second one, she was careful to wash the glass and put it back with the others.

CHAPTER ELEVEN

Patrini's wasn't fancy, but it had the greatest Italian food in town. It was absolutely Holly's favorite place to eat. She licked her lips, scanning the menu from top to bottom. "I wish this was like one of those Chinese places, where you get a little bit of everything."

She ordered her favorite: lasagna, with clams on the half-shell as an appetizer.

"So how do you think the cheer competition stacks up?" Holly's mom asked between bites.

"Miss Connors says in all the years she's coached cheer squads, we're the best she's had. She even thinks we look better than the seniors!" Holly got a hopeful look in her eye. "Can you imagine if *we* won our division and the senior team didn't win? Cindy would lie down on her pom-poms and die!"

"Is she still giving you a hard time?" Holly's mom asked.

Her voice became sad. "Yeah. Last week in study hall she walked out the door in front of me and slammed it right in my face. She pushed it so hard I dropped my books."

"That's awful!" her father said.

"She also started a rumor that I was after Kevin. The worst part is, Sandy *believes* her! I don't even like Kevin that much. . . ."

"How could Sandy believe that? She should know better."

"Cindy's been hanging around all my friends. She even asked Melissa and Sandy to a makeup party she had. She's turning them all against me."

"Well, they're not very good friends if they hang around with her, knowing what she's doing. You girls have been friends for years. How could they let someone like her come between you?"

Holly rested her fork on her plate. For a psychologist, her mom was pretty stupid. "She's *popular*, Mom!"

"I have trouble understanding how someone so mean can be popular."

"You should know kids, Mom. You counsel them all day long. She's pretty, and she's got great clothes. Because she acts like she's so special, everyone thinks she is. The boys want to date her, and the girls want to look like her. It's really not so complicated."

"Well, maybe she'll get tired of picking on you," Holly's father offered.

"She told me she wished she wasn't graduating because she'd like to be around another year to make my life miserable!" Holly poked at her food. "I try to avoid her, but she goes out of her way to find me. Today she walked by our lunch table and 'accidentally' bumped my elbow as I was drinking my orange juice.

170

It spilled all over my shirt, and I had to walk around like that the rest of the day. It was so embarrassing."

"I can imagine."

There was an awkward silence, as if they'd forgotten how to speak to each other. And there was an unidentifiable tension in the air. Holly's dad had been unusually quiet all day and seemed really depressed ever since he came home. There was something wrong, and Holly knew it.

"It's been a long time since we had a nice dinner together," her father said.

"Yes, it has." Holly's mom smiled and raised her wine glass. "We'll have to do it more often."

Holly sipped her iced tea. "Daddy, could I have a glass of wine?"

"Wine? You?"

"Just one . . . to toast Mom's new show."

He guessed it was okay. No one would question her age. He looked to his wife for approval. "Why not? I'd say we've got reason to celebrate."

As they toasted Dr. Carol's success, Holly had to restrain her impulse to empty the glass in one gulp. She paced herself, taking only quick sips until it was gone. She expected to feel better once she finished it, but she didn't. One glass was never enough anymore. She longed to have another.

She wondered if she should tell them about Billy and how concerned she was. Now that they were finally together, was it a good time to tell them that she was failing two of her classes? Or to ask her mother how she could get Jeff back?

Most of all, Holly fought her desire to tell her parents

171

what had happened at the homecoming dance—as if telling it would make it go away.

Her face grew sad when she realized that, no matter what she did or said, nothing could ever erase the memory of that horrible night. There were no tapes, no glues, no nails or tools that could repair the damage she'd done to her own reputation.

"You look so sad," her father said. "What's going through that beautiful head of yours?"

Now, she had tears in her eyes. Would they still love her if she told them, or would they be disgusted by her? Would they be sympathetic, or merely angered by her stupidity and irresponsibility? She just couldn't be sure, and she didn't want to risk spoiling this evening in order to find out.

"Holly, you look like you're about to cry! What's wrong?"

"I guess I'm just worried about Billy." It wasn't all of the truth, but it was part of it.

"What about him?"

"He's sick."

"With what?"

"I . . . I don't know. He's losing weight. He says he can't keep food down. He gets really bad stomach pains and nosebleeds. It happened twice when I was with him, and Kevin said it happened again yesterday when they were playing basketball. Only yesterday it was worse—Billy passed out cold! He looks funny—kind of yellowish. . . ."

The expression on her mother's face told her that something must be terribly wrong. Billy was *really* sick. Holly had sensed it all along.

172

Mrs. Henderson glanced at her husband.

After careful consideration, Holly's dad said to his wife, "I think you should tell her."

"Tell me what?"

Holly's mother chose her words carefully. She knew how they would hurt. "Holly, do you remember a few years ago when Billy's mother died?"

"Of course I do. Everyone remembers that."

"Do you remember how she died?"

"Pneumonia. She had pneumonia."

"Well, that's what they told everyone, but that's really not what she had." She sipped her wine thoughtfully before she continued. "Holly, Billy's mother died of alcoholism, not pneumonia."

"I don't believe that. It can't be true."

"Yes, it's true. Dr. Halverson did the autopsy. He told us. That's why we've always been so concerned about the way Billy drinks."

Now it all made perfect sense to Holly. Billy's mom was always moody. One minute she'd be laughing and carrying on, the next she'd be hollering at the kids to get out of the house.

Holly remembered a time when she was only six or seven. She and Billy had camped out in his back yard, and his mother made them breakfast. That morning Billy's mother had beer with her pancakes. . . . In fact, now that Holly thought about it, she recalled that Billy's mother always had a drink in her hand. Holly had just assumed it was iced tea or a soft drink.

Billy's dad drank heavily, everyone knew that. Alcohol was usually the cause of his violence. But no one knew about his mother. . . .

"Oh my gosh," Holly said, "poor Billy! I can't believe he never told me. How come *you* never told me?"

Then, the horrifying reality hit her, but she denied it out loud. "Billy's not an alcoholic."

"Holly, he's been drinking since he was eight years old!"

"But he hardly ever gets drunk!"

"Alcoholics seldom do. Their tolerance for liquor is so high they often seem as normal as you or I." Holly's mom stopped herself from sounding too clinical.

"I counsel alcoholics nearly every day. I've always been concerned about Billy. If he wasn't so dependent on you, I would have discouraged any involvement with him. But Billy needs you. He needs your support. And since you don't drink, you can be an example for him."

Holly's thoughts turned from Billy to herself. "Lots of kids drink, Mom."

"And a lot of kids become alcoholics. It happens every day. It sounds to me like Billy has a liver problem. He's got all the symptoms: loss of appetite and weight, nausea, jaundice—that's the yellowish look you described in his skin. And nosebleeds are a symptom, too. Holly, Billy has to get professional help. If he doesn't quit drinking, he'll kill himself."

"Kill himself . . . kill himself." Holly heard the words over and over. She couldn't imagine life without Billy. She stared at her plate, concerned for Billy and concerned for herself. "Can we go?"

Mr. Henderson glanced at his watch. "It's only 10:15. I thought you girls might enjoy a late movie."

"No, Daddy. I just wanna go home."

174

CHAPTER TWELVE

Holly was lying on her bed, trying to go over the cheer routines in her head. No matter how she tried, she couldn't concentrate. All she could think of was Billy.

She slipped on her robe and went to the kitchen for a glass of milk. When she flicked on the light, she found her father sitting alone at the table.

"You scared me, Daddy. Why are you sitting in the dark?"

His face was drawn and sad. "I lost my job," he said attempting a weak smile. "I couldn't sleep."

She pulled out a chair and sat beside him. "Oh, Daddy, that's awful. I'm so sorry. Does Mom know?"

"I was going to tell you both at dinner tonight, but we were having such a nice time I didn't want to spoil it."

"Are you okay?"

Now, he smiled more sincerely. "Yeah, I really am. It wasn't as bad as I thought it would be. I guess the good Lord prepared me for it."

She'd never heard either of her parents refer to the "Lord" before. All of a sudden, she thought about that day in the park, when Billy talked to her about God.

"I've been sitting here thinking. It's true what you said on the phone a couple of weeks ago. Since Mom's career took off, the three of us haven't spent much time together. I've missed that."

"Me, too."

He leaned over and kissed her cheek. "I know you have. I was getting sick of Hollywood anyway. The job was okay, but I hated all the stuff that went with it. . . . Ah, you don't want to hear about that." He pushed his words away.

"Anyway, I was thinking that if I got a local job—maybe teaching at the university—we could have more time together, and I could get all the stuff done around here that your mother's been nagging me to do. Don't you dare tell her I said that! Want some milk?"

He took the pitcher from the refrigerator and filled two glasses. "Want a cookie?"

"No thanks."

He took one for himself. "So, how come you're up so late?"

"I couldn't sleep either."

"Too much lasagna?"

"No, I've just got a lot on my mind."

"Like what?"

"Oh, like Billy, I guess, and the cheer competition tomorrow morning."

"Oh my gosh, is that tomorrow already?"

176

"It can't come soon enough for me! I just want it over with. I'm so sick of those routines I could spit. We've been doing the same routines over and over for eight weeks."

"Can Mom and I watch?"

"No!"

He flinched as the word rang through his ear.

She noticed the look of alarm on his face and softened her voice. "I mean, I wish you wouldn't. . . . I'm nervous enough already."

"I'd say that's obvious."

"I didn't mean to shout. It's just that this is the first time in eighteen years Kennedy High's made it to the semi-finals. Miss Connors acts like it's the World Series or something. She's putting a tremendous amount of pressure on us to win—and on me in particular. She's always going on about how I'm her best dancer and they can't win without me. It's like she'll hold me personally responsible if we lose."

Holly's father noticed excitement in her voice. But it wasn't a good sound. It was laced with nervousness and anxiety. She began talking louder and faster, and her hands were trembling.

"Everything's been unreal for me lately! There's Cindy . . . she's on my back all the time! This stupid competition is driving me crazy. My grades are going down the sewer, and everything's going wrong at school. Sandy hates me, and Jeff doesn't like me . . . and now Billy! I just feel like I'm coming apart. I don't think I can handle it anymore! I don't think I can take a single second more of this!"

She jumped up and stood over her father, pleading

177

with him, "I need a drink, Daddy! I need a drink to calm my nerves!" Her hands shook harder, and she began to cry.

Mr. Henderson's eyes narrowed as he stared up at his daughter. "Holly! What's wrong with you?"

"Everything! Everything's wrong with me!"

He'd never seen her like this—never suspected that she was anything but an ideal kid. He thought about their dinner conversation and about Billy in particular . . . and about Holly's friendship with him.

"Did you mean that? You feel you *need* a drink?"

She looked him squarely in the eye and wiped the tears from her cheeks. "Yes."

"Oh, Holly," he said sadly. So that was it . . . Holly was drinking right along with Billy. He stood up, pulling her to him, and wrapped his arms around her. "It'll be all right, baby. Everything will be all right." He held her until she fell asleep.

When Holly's alarm sounded at five-thirty, she turned off the clock radio and went back to sleep.

At six o'clock, she woke with a start and sat bolt upright in bed. "Oh my gosh," she said aloud. "It's after six!" She jumped out of bed and ran to the shower.

The cheer competition didn't start until eight, but it was a forty-five-minute bus ride to the civic center where the competition was being held. She was supposed to meet Lindsey at the bus stop at 6:30. They were to report by 7:15 so they'd have time to go through the routines once before the contest began. She rushed to get ready and ran out the door fifteen minutes late.

Her telephone was ringing as she left, but she was too late to stop and answer it. She just pulled her door shut so the ringing wouldn't waken her parents.

As she approached the civic center grounds from the bus stop, Lindsey and Christine came running toward her.

"Where were you last night? We tried to call you until after ten!"

"I went out to dinner with my parents. What's wrong?"

"I tried to call you this morning, and then when you weren't at the bus stop. . . ."

"I got up late. What's the matter?"

They exchanged glances. "Just tell her, Lins," Christine said sadly.

Lindsey's brow was furrowed with worry. She looked over her shoulder at the other Kennedy cheerleaders, who were all standing in the background, watching to see Holly's reaction. "Holly. . . ." Lindsey was obviously nervous, and she kept glancing over her shoulder.

"What's going on?" Holly demanded.

"They . . . Miss Connors . . . I tried to call you last night to save you the embarrassment of coming down here. . . . Miss Connors kicked you off the cheer squad because you're failing two classes. You can't compete. The board says if you participate, we have to forfeit the competition."

Holly was mortified. She looked over Lindsey's shoulder. The first face she saw was Cindy's. She was smiling sarcastically, and she gave a little wave of her white-gloved hand.

Lindsey was staring at the grass. "Miss Connors

179

didn't get the notice from the superintendent until after school yesterday."

Holly threw her pom-poms on the grass and ran toward the bus stop.

Lindsey ran after her. "Holly, wait! Please wait!"

Holly collapsed on the bench, crying.

"Don't worry, Holly. It doesn't matter! You'll get your grades back up, and you can try out again next year. Holly, please don't cry!"

Holly took off her glove so she wouldn't get mascara on it when she wiped her face. "I'll be okay. You'd better get back. . . ."

"Are you sure?"

"Yeah, I'm sure. I'll call you later. Good luck, Lins!" she called after her.

In addition to everything else, Holly was certain that if they didn't win, everyone in the sophomore class would blame her.

❖ ❖ ❖

When Holly got off the bus at Meeker Street, it wasn't even eight o'clock yet. She couldn't go home because then she'd have to explain everything to her parents, and she knew she couldn't handle that.

She walked around the park until she got hungry. She had two dollars in her purse, so she went to a fast-food restaurant to get some breakfast.

Taking the bag of food outside, she sat on the curb and opened it. Just the smell of it made her sick. She was too nervous and upset to eat. She tossed it in a trash can and started down Howard Street toward Billy's house.

Billy's dad was just pulling out of the driveway as

she approached the house. She waited until his car disappeared around the corner, then she went up to the house and rang the doorbell. When Billy didn't answer, she knocked hard. Finally, she walked around the side of the house to his bedroom window.

The kids always joked about how Billy could sleep through earthquakes and tornados. More than a few times, he'd embarrassed himself by snoring in class. Once, he even fell asleep during a roller-coaster ride.

She peeked inside his window. He was asleep in bed, his feet sticking out of the covers. He didn't move when she tapped on the window, so she walked around to the back door and let herself in.

She nudged him gently, afraid she'd startle him. "Billy? Billy, wake up. I've gotta talk to you."

He didn't move, so she shook him harder. When he still didn't move, she pulled the pillow from underneath his head and hit him with it. When that didn't work, she went for his feet.

She crept toward the end of the bed, taking a pencil from his desk on the way. That's when she noticed the Bible. She opened it and read the inscription: "For Billy. Someday I'll be gone, but God's Word will live forever. With all my love, Grandma." Next to the inscription, Billy's grandmother had penned a verse from the Bible:

"I am the light of the world. Whoever follows me will never walk in darkness, but will have the light of life." (John 8:12)

Laying on the desk was a Polaroid photograph of a little boy in a wheelchair. He was horribly crippled, and his head was bent to one side. Billy was next to him, smiling. Holly picked it up and looked closer. The little brown dog from the toy store was on the boy's lap. Holly smiled at the thought of Billy and the little boy and wondered why he had kept the friendship secret. Carefully, she set the picture back in its place, feeling guilty that she had invaded some very personal parts of Billy's life.

She walked to the end of the bed and slowly ran the cold pencil lead over the bottom of his foot. There was a reflex action, but nothing much. She began to giggle as she did it again, a little harder this time. He twitched his foot spastically. The sudden movement scared her, and she jumped backward, laughing.

Then, she snatched up his foot. She giggled playfully as she held it tightly with one hand and tickled him with the other.

At once, some instinct warned her. Without realizing it, she moved her hand up his calf and held it there, squeezing his flesh. Then, with a sudden, horrified jerk, she released his leg and jumped. Billy's body was cold . . . and clammy!

She ran to the head of the bed and threw back the covers. He was white. And his lips were blue. She screamed and began shaking him, then slapped his face. She flipped his body over and put her hand on his chest. When she couldn't feel a pulse, she ran to the phone and dialed 911.

CHAPTER THIRTEEN

Holly was still in her cheerleading uniform when she looked up the long, narrow hospital corridor and saw her mother and father coming toward her.

"What happened?"

Holly fell into her mother's arms. "Oh, Mom, it was awful! I was tickling Billy's feet. I thought he was asleep. . . . Then I felt his leg, and I thought he was *dead!*"

"Where is he now?"

"They took him into surgery. I couldn't find his pulse!"

"Have they notified his father?"

"No one knows where he is."

Hospital noises echoed eerily through the corridors. Footsteps, telephones pulsing, the voice over the loudspeaker: "Paging Dr. Walsh . . . Dr. Walsh to Emergency, stat!"

Candy stripers rolled steel carts down the hallways, offering magazines and snacks to patients in hospital gowns. Nurses chatted merrily, as if Billy were

183

perfectly fine. She heard someone weeping. . . . And there was the smell—that horrible hospital smell of sickness . . . and death.

They waited as minutes turned into hours, and still, the doctor had not come to talk to them.

Holly's mother and father sat on each side of her, offering comfort in vain.

"T. J., do you think you should try his father at home again?"

"I just called ten minutes ago. There's still no answer."

Holly twisted a worn Kleenex nervously in her hands. "Is he going to die, Daddy?"

He looked to his wife, as if she had some mystical power to know the answer. "I don't know, honey. We won't know anything until the doctor comes out."

Holly's mom began pacing the floor in front of the bench where they were sitting. "I knew he was a heavy drinker. I should have seen this coming. I should have done something."

Holly glared at her. "*What?* And take time away from your precious radio show?"

"Holly, what an awful thing to say to your mother! You apologize."

"No, I won't. It's true. That could be *me* lying in that bed, and you'd never even know it! The only way I could get your attention is if I called you at the station and said, 'Hey, Dr. Carol, help me. I'm having a crisis!'"

"Holly, stop it!"

She jumped up, stomping her foot. "No, I won't! I won't stop! You deserve it—you *both* deserve it!" She

184

turned on her father. "And you! If you hadn't gotten fired from your job, you wouldn't even be here. You'd probably be out at the mini-market signing autographs. That's more important to you than Billy or me or anything else!"

Holly started down the corridor and then turned back, shouting loud enough to startle everyone waiting for the elevator. "You just better not let anything happen to Billy!" Her teeth were clenched tightly, her chest was heaving. She felt stupid for what she'd said, as if anyone—especially her parents—had any control over Billy's destiny. . . . She flung open the door to the stairwell and ran down the five flights of stairs and out to the street.

Emotionally stunned, Holly's parents stared after her. When T. J. Henderson finally looked into his wife's eyes, he saw that she was crying.

"Is it true, T. J.? Did you lose your job?"

"Yesterday. I was going to tell you. I just never got around to it. . . . I was up late last night and so was Holly. We had a talk, and I told her then."

He took her hand. "Let's go get some coffee."

He told his wife everything that Holly had told him the night before, and added his speculation that Holly had a drinking problem.

"You know, I thought the liquor was disappearing," Carol said. "And when I came home the night she was chosen homecoming princess, she was drunk. She told me she'd been celebrating. I didn't think much of it, because I knew she was upset with me for not taking her shopping." She shook her head negatively, awed by her own stupidity. "I thought her drinking was just a

185

way of getting back at me. It was obvious she wanted me to find out. Oh, I'm so stupid!"

She hung her head, disgusted with herself for her insensitivity. "Holly told me I was never there when she needed me. Oh, T. J.," she said sadly, "I should have seen it then. All the signs were there. She's been sneaking out at night, disobeying every rule. Her grades have been slipping miserably, and she's developed this flippant attitude that I've never seen in her.

"I knew Billy had a serious problem. I should have done something for him. Instead, I ignored the problem when it was right in my own back yard. I should have been watching their friendship more closely. I never worried about Holly. She's always been so involved with her cheerleading and activities at school. . . . She's always appeared so self-sufficient!"

Carol sipped her coffee, but it felt like rocks when she tried to swallow. "Holly's always been such an ideal kid. I never even suspected that she had a drinking problem! Now, it's all so clear to me. . . . All these months, she's felt rejected and alone—as if we'd deserted her. She tried to tell us about all the pressure she's been under, and we just dismissed her. I didn't give most of what she said a second thought."

T. J. reached across the table and gently touched his wife's hand. "You can't blame yourself. It's my fault, too. I wasn't there for her either. Here, wipe your nose." He handed her a hankerchief.

"Holly's always seemed so grown up," he continued. "Remember when she was eight and she insisted on riding the city bus to Grandma's all by herself? Remember how indignant she was when we told her she was too

186

little?" He smiled at the recollection.

"She'd never let me help her with anything," Carol said. "She used to button her dress all the way up the back and try to slip it over her head so she wouldn't have to ask for help. When she got her hair caught, she'd holler until I thought they could hear her at the deli!

"We both let her down. But I'm a psychologist, for heaven's sake! I'm supposed to be trained to know how painful adolescence can be. When my own daughter needed me most, I wasn't there.

"She's right, you know, about my job. It *has* been the most important thing to me. I've been so distant, I didn't even know my own husband lost his job. . . ."

A unfamiliar voice interrupted her. When they looked up, the doctor was standing over them. "Are you the people who brought the boy in?"

"Our daughter did. She's not here right now. How is he?"

"Have you located his family?"

"We've tried the house several times, but no one answers. It's only his father. His mother's dead. How's Billy?"

"He's not good. He's been recovering from surgery, and now he's awake in his room. The liver is damaged beyond repair. The boy's suffering from severe cirrhosis."

"*Cirrhosis?* In a young boy?" T. J. asked.

"It's rare," the doctor responded, "but it happens. In this case, the boy's liver was already damaged. He may have been in an automobile accident, or possibly he received a hard blow to the stomach. It's difficult to tell what happened, but his liver was already very weak. The drinking just accelerated the scarring and loss of function. You can see him, but not for long. You better do everything you can to find his father. I'm sorry."

❖ ❖ ❖

Holly sat alone on the curb outside the emergency room entrance. She couldn't explain it, but she felt a deep longing to be with Jeff, to be comforted by him. She knew Billy liked him, and she thought that Jeff's being there would make Billy feel better. She dug in her purse and pulled out a quarter. With a shaky finger, she managed to dial Jeff's number.

"Jeff, please don't hang up. This is Holly. . . ."

She could almost hear the smile in his voice when he spoke. "Hi, Holly. Why would I want to hang up? What's going on?"

"Jeff . . ." she began to cry into the phone.

"Holly, what's the matter? What happened?"

"It's Billy! I'm at the hospital. I had to bring him to the emergency room. He's having an operation, and he's really sick. Would you . . . do you think you could come over?"

After Jeff reassured her, she plopped down on the curb outside the emergency entrance to wait for him. She heard her mother's voice behind her, "Is this seat taken?"

Holly looked up. "No. If you can stand to sit next to me, it's all yours."

"I think it should be the other way around. Can you stand to sit beside me?"

188

Holly wrapped her arms around her mom's neck. "I didn't mean all those things I said, Mom! I'm sorry," she sobbed.

She held her daughter tightly. "I'm the one who's sorry. I should have paid more attention. I've been selfish, and I don't even have an excuse for myself.

"I got so caught up in my career and what I wanted, I lost sight of what's really important—you and Dad. I'm sorry for the last six months, Holly. I'm sorry I wasn't here to help you through this awful time you're having. . . ."

"Oh, Mom, I've messed up everything! I got kicked off the cheer squad today!"

As a psychologist, Carol was well trained in ways to keep her shock and dismay from being obvious. She simply asked, "Why? What happened?"

"I'm failing science and algebra. I showed up for the competition this morning, and right in front of Cindy and everyone, Lindsey told me I was off the squad! I was so embarrassed!"

"It must have been awful for you."

"It was. But it was nothing compared to some of the stuff I've done lately. Last weekend at the homecoming dance, I got so drunk I made a total fool out of myself in front of everyone in the whole school!

"There I was, a homecoming princess, and everyone in the whole student body was laughing at me and calling me a lush. It was humiliating beyond belief! Now everyone hates me."

"Everyone doesn't hate you!"

"Well, everyone avoids me, at least. I hear them talking. . . . And Jeff doesn't want to go out with me

189

anymore. I feel like everyone's talking about me behind my back. And Cindy called me a lush right to my face! Everyone thinks I have a drinking problem—even Lindsey!"

"Do you?"

"Do I what?"

"Do you have a drinking problem?"

It was a question Holly never expected. She avoided her mother's eyes. She thought about lying, but that would only make things worse. "I feel like I can't get through the day without a drink," she said honestly. "Especially now. It doesn't matter what I do from now on, everyone will remember what a fool I made of myself. I'll never live it down!"

Carol stretched out her arms. "Come here, baby."

She fell into her mother's arms, sobbing. "Oh Mom, I'm so sorry for everything! I don't know what happened. All of a sudden, everything just went wrong!

"I used to love school. I loved cheerleading and dancing and seeing my friends. I didn't even mind homework. Then all this mess started because I liked Jeff. It was like I was at the bottom of a snowy hill, and my problems were like a snowball rolling down toward me, getting bigger and bigger. By the time they reached me, they just rolled over me and left me flat. And you weren't there. I didn't have anyone to talk to.

"The alcohol seemed to make things all right again. I felt good when I drank—happy. I didn't care if Cindy was talking behind my back or if she was turning other people against me. If I got drunk enough, I could forget about the humiliation I felt at being tripped or having soda poured all over me.

"Sometimes, I drank so that I could just go to sleep. . . . Oh, Mom, I hate myself for what I've done!"

"Don't do that, Holly. Don't hate yourself. It won't solve anything. What's done can't be undone or changed. We love you, no matter what's happened. You made some mistakes, but everyone does that."

"Yeah, but no one does it as good as me!"

"I don't know. I've made some pretty miserable mistakes myself. Listen, we'll talk more later." She helped Holly up. "Billy's awake. The doctor said you can see him, but only for a little while."

As they started through the large double doors, they saw Jeff approaching from the other side of the lobby. He had on his blue letterman's sweater.

He held out a hand to Holly's mother. "Hi, I'm Jeff Reynolds."

"Hi, Jeff, I'm Carol Henderson, Holly's mom. Listen, why don't the two of you go up and see Billy? Dad and I will wait in the coffee shop. Come get us if you need us."

❖ ❖ ❖

Billy had tubes running into his nose and arms. His eyes were shut, but he opened them when he sensed someone standing over him. "Hi," he said weakly.

"Hi, yourself," Holly said.

"I guess I did it this time, didn't I?"

"Yeah, I guess you did. Jeff's here with me." She pointed toward the door.

Billy struggled to look past her, but he couldn't lift his head from the pillow.

Jeff stood near the door. He wanted to be there

191

for Holly, but he didn't want to interfere. He smiled at Billy. "Hey, buddy!"

Billy responded weakly, "Hey." He tried to raise himself up so he could see his arms. "Did you glue all these tubes on me?" he teased.

"No, not this time."

"I feel lousy."

"You look lousy." There were dark circles under his eyes, and his lips were a chalky white.

"I feel like I'm going to die."

"You are . . . when you're a hundred and seven."

His eyes were deeply sunken and appeared to be glazed over. His voice was frail. "I don't think so, I keep . . . like floating back and forth. I think . . . I'm really dying."

She stared at him, paralyzed by his statement and the certainty with which he made it. "Don't say that!"

"I'm not afraid." He sounded peaceful—almost elated—and it horrified her.

"Billy, please stop it! It sounds so spooky!"

He smiled faintly. "Not spooky . . . beautiful. Kind of like . . ." his voice trailed off.

"Billy," she cried, "you're scaring me!" She backed away, as if a greater distance between them would take away the reality of the moment. "Don't say stuff like that!" she insisted. "Jeff, did you hear what he said?" She couldn't control her emotions. She began to cry.

Jeff felt helpless. Every instinct he had told him that this was for real. Billy was going to die. There was nothing he could say or do to change that. He went beside Holly and put his arm around her shoulders. "Don't cry, Holly," he said gently.

192

She turned to Jeff, horror on her face. "Jeff, I'm scared! Can't we do anything to help him?" The tears were coming harder now, rolling one after the other down her cheeks like crystal beads torn from a string. "I'm going to get the doctor!" she said impulsively.

"No," Billy said, "please, don't leave me!"

Jeff prayed silently for the right words to say. He couldn't remember ever feeling so inadequate. He took Holly's hand and squeezed it tightly—a gesture that told her to be strong.

Billy sensed her suffering. He wanted to hold Holly and comfort her, but his arms were too weak. He managed to pat the bed. "Sit here."

Apprehensively, she sat down, careful not to disturb the tubes and bottles.

When Billy looked at her, his eyes were full of pain. He spoke slowly, so she would remember every word. "People don't love each other enough. They don't see when someone hurts. . . . They don't care when someone's lonely or sick. . . ."

"Oh, Billy!" She turned helplessly to Jeff.

Jeff's heart began to pound as the gravity of the situation overwhelmed him. He'd never experienced anything like this before. He'd never been so close to death. He fought to keep his composure. "It's okay, Holly."

He walked to the other side of the bed and stood over Billy. He felt a lump swelling up inside his throat as he struggled to keep a sound of confidence in his voice. He put his hand on Billy's. "Remember that day we went out for a hamburger and we talked about Jesus? We talked a long time about Him. Do you remember that?"

193

"Yeah."

"You told me that you were ready to follow Him. Did you really mean what you said?"

Billy's voice was weak, but he responded without hesitation. "Yes, I'm ready to follow Him. I told you I read the Bible sometimes. It says if we believe in Jesus we'll live forever." He sat up, the bottles and tubes no hindrance to him now. "*Forever*, Holly, think of it! I know Jesus is here with me now."

There was an urgency in Billy's eyes unlike anything Holly had ever seen. She was no longer frightened; she was mesmerized. She pushed him gently back onto his pillow.

"I know so many things now," he continued. "All this stuff I read in the Bible, all the stories my grandma told me. . . ." Though his voice was frail, it was filled with excitement over the things he finally understood so clearly. "My grandma used to talk about Jesus. She read Bible stories to me." He closed his eyes, imagining the quiet security he felt while in his grandmother's lap, feeling the warmth of her arms around his small body. He could hear echos of her soft, sweet voice as she lovingly read to him. When he opened his eyes, they were filled with tears. He spoke slowly, his words laden with sadness. "After she died, no one told me about Jesus anymore. No one read me stories."

He looked directly into Holly's eyes and smiled at her. "I'll see my grandma, Holly. I know it!"

He began coughing, gasping for breath. Jeff lifted his head and said, "Do you want the doctor?"

"No." Billy closed his eyes. "I'm so tired. My eyes won't stay open. . . ."

194

"Just rest," Jeff said, "we'll talk later. We'll stay right here."

But Billy wasn't ready to stop. Not until he told Holly everything he knew. "Listen, Holly. Don't worry about things at school. I know it seems important now, but if you were here—where I am—you'd understand. It's really not so important."

He closed his eyes again. "Does my dad know I'm here?"

"He's not home," Holly said.

"He has a new girlfriend . . . Suzie."

"We'll keep trying 'til we find him."

"I'm so tired. They gave me medicine for the pain. I feel funny . . . like I'm part sleeping and part awake. Poor Pete. He won't know what happened to me."

Holly kept looking toward the door. She wanted to run, but grief held her like chains to Billy's bed. She took a wet cloth from the bedside tray. "I'm going to wipe your forehead. It'll feel nice," she said quietly.

Outwardly, she appeared calm as she wiped Billy's brow with the cool, soft cloth. But inside, her pores prickled with foreboding as every sense she possessed told her that he was really, truly going to die. There was nothing, no one, that could save him. . . .

Billy turned to Jeff. "Thanks for comin' over. And thanks for caring about me. Could I be alone with Holly for a minute?"

"Sure. I'll wait outside."

Billy reached for her hand and covered it with his. "I love you, Hol. I love my dad, too. I just never told him that. I know you'll miss me, but don't be sad."

"Billy. . . ."

"Don't cry, just listen. Promise you won't laugh."

"I promise," she sniffed.

"I know a Bible verse," he said proudly. "Now listen: God 'will wipe every tear from their eyes. There will be no more death or mourning or crying or pain, for the old order of things has passed away,' Revelation twenty-one, verse four."

"It's beautiful."

"That's what it's like . . . with Jesus. Can you imagine? No more death, no crying or pain." There was a distant look in his eyes. "No one hitting you. No one telling you you're worthless. No crying, no pain . . . only happiness."

The truth was, she couldn't imagine it, but she wanted to. She tucked the sheets under his chin, bent, and kissed him softly. "I'll sit here, right by your bed. You rest now."

"I see Him!"

"What?"

Billy's voice was barely audible. "I see Jesus!"

Horrified, she watched Billy close his eyes for the last time. Alone next to his bed, she buried her head in her hands and wept. "Oh, God," she pleaded, "what'll I do without my Billy?"

CHAPTER FOURTEEN

Holly's mom was sitting on the couch reading when Holly came down the stairs. It was almost noon, and she was still in her pajamas.

"Can I talk to you, Mom?"

She closed her book immediately. "Of course, honey. Do you want anything?"

"No, thanks." She sat on the couch close to her mother. "Mom, do you believe in God?"

"Of course I do."

"Do you think God caused Billy to die?"

"No. I think God allowed it—maybe because He knew Billy would be happier with Him—but He didn't make it happen. I don't think God makes bad things happen."

"How come we don't go to church anymore?"

Her mom's answer took some thought. "I think we got so busy, we let our priorities get out of whack. Sunday's the only day of the week that one of us didn't have to get up and go someplace. I guess we just got lazy."

"Do you think we could start going again?"

"Well, I suppose. . . ."

"Since you've decided to quit your practice and just do the radio show, you'll have a lot more time at home. And if Daddy gets the teaching job at the university, you'll both have weekends off. You could sleep in on Saturdays."

Holly's mom hesitated. She believed in God, but going to church didn't seem to be a priority. Until now.

"Well, Mom, what do you think?"

"It sounds really important to you."

"I had a long talk with Jeff after Billy's funeral, and I . . . Mom, I prayed to Jesus. I was thinking that maybe we could start going to church. You know . . . as a family? I'd really like to go. I think I'd like to know God better."

She smiled, giving her daughter a hug. "I think it would be good for all of us."

"Thanks, Mom."

"How are you feeling today?"

"I think I'm ready to go back to school now."

"Are you sure?"

"Yes, I'm sure. It's been over a week since Billy's funeral. I can't avoid them forever."

"It won't be easy."

"I know. But I think I can handle it." Inside, Holly knew she could handle it. She was armed with a new strength, a brand-new reason for living.

For Holly Henderson, the old order of things had passed away. It was time for her to get on with her new life.

AUTHOR

Lynn Stanley was born in Minnesota but raised in Southern California. She received a degree from Rio Hondo College in Whittier, California, before traveling through Europe at the age of eighteen.

Lynn married Fred Stanley in 1968. Fred played professional baseball (mostly with the New York Yankees) for the first eighteen years of their marriage. He now coaches for the Seattle Mariners.

They have two teenage children—Traci and B. J.—and have lived in Arizona for twenty-three years, returning to their home in Scottsdale after the baseball season every year.

Lynn has been a freelance writer for nine years and has published many articles in regional publications. She and Fred collaborated on *The Complete Instructional Baseball Manual,* which they self-published in 1987. *The Manual* is available in bookstores and has been translated into Japanese.